RESCUE 2050

Let your heart rejoice
Let your flesh also rest in
hope   Ps 16:9 (paraphrased)

Enjoy the Story
Dorothy
Feb 2018

DOROTHY SEKABIRA

ISBN: 1975682300
ISBN 13: 9781975682309
Library of Congress Control Number: 2017913324
CreateSpace Independent Publishing Platform
North Charleston, South Carolina

ACKNOWLEDGEMENTS:

It is impossible to express the full measure of gratitude to everyone who played a part in bringing this book together.

First and foremost I am thankful to my family and friends who have encouraged and cheered for me as a new author.

Many thanks for those who believed in this book and spent time reading my manuscript: Charlene, Chris, Courtney, Dorece, Favour, John, Laurie, Mark, Regan, Stephanie, Sherry, Shirley, Tim, Todd and Wally.

There will be great earthquakes in various places.

Luke 21:11

TABLE OF CONTENTS

Prologue   ix

Chapter 1   1
Chapter 2   5
Chapter 3   9
Chapter 4   15
Chapter 5   20
Chapter 6   26
Chapter 7   29
Chapter 8   33
Chapter 9   39
Chapter 10   44
Chapter 11   47
Chapter 12   50
Chapter 13   53
Chapter 14   65
Chapter 15   69
Chapter 16   72
Chapter 17   78
Chapter 18   81
Chapter 19   87
Chapter 20   95

Chapter 21   98

Chapter 22   104

Chapter 23   107

Chapter 24   110

Prologue

From deep within the earth's core, a tremor quickly raced up through miles of the mantle. Erupting across the redwood-forest floor, its call violently shook the thick roots of the ancient trees, before vibrating up the tall trunks to tease loose leaves from their branches.

⅄

The new era of artificial intelligence, or AI, was in full swing in 2050. Machines were on their way to better reasoning, collaborating, and even imagining. A decade earlier, scientists had created algorithms that improved the decision-making ability of computers, causing an acceleration in the ease of applying automation to everything. As AI exploded across the world, the need for satellites to govern this work increased. Nations scrambled for space dominance in the lower Earth orbit. More satellites were added each year, until the mass of metal in orbit had grown to an unfathomable amount, mirroring the increasing garbage piling up on Earth's surface.

The International Board of Space Safety Engineers watched the overcrowded space with great anxiety as they worked feverishly to come up with solutions to avert the inevitable catastrophe: the dreaded domino effect. It would take just a single debris shower moving within the packed stratosphere to damage multiple satellites and cause blackouts across the globe.

Into this new reality of shared space, the global unions enforced a rule that every new satellite launched come with a counter-debris system. These offensive weapons vacuumed stray debris particles before they turned into agents of destruction. At the moment, however, there was no such impeding danger; every satellite hummed along perfectly, some more active than others.

One in particular was working overtime. This was the main satellite of the Earthquake Robotics Company, in short, known as ERC. It was the implementation arm of the Search and Rescue Unit of the United States Disaster Response Division. Currently, the ERC satellite's output was focused on one area in Asia: Muyang, Thailand. Less than seventy-two hours previously, the city had been bustling with nightlife. Now it lay in shambles; a graveyard of fallen towers and bleeding bodies, the quick work of a massive quake, which, unfortunately, was an all too common occurrence in this present era.

CHAPTER 1

A Roboman stepped onto a mound of earthquake debris. A simulacrum of a man fashioned in metal, pistons, and gears instead of bone, blood, and muscle and built with powerful legs to effortlessly balance its weight on the unstable ground it now searched. Walking, stopping to beam a laser down into the layers of darkness below to collect and analyze data, and then move on.

A few moments later, a series of several quick beeps sounded off from its systems, indication of a heat source under its feet. Carefully it bent down to brush the debris aside, revealing a half-buried car in the dirt. Effortlessly it ripped off the roof, exposing a man lying facedown in the backseat. The Roboman reached down and felt for a pulse on the neck of the victim— nothing. It then rolled the man aside, revealing a teenage girl badly bruised and caked in mud, but very much alive.

Overcome with the relief of being found, the girl grabbed the Roboman's hand, only to feel cold and unyielding metal. She shrank back, hyperventilating. Desperately looking around for cover, she tried unsuccessfully to crawl back under the dead man and then cried out in agony as pain shot through her battered body. She squeezed her eyes shut, wishing the nightmare away, but the metal monster was still there when she opened them again. As the robot bent down closer to her, the girl cried out in terror.

"Let me talk to her," said a voice behind the Roboman.

His name-tag read "Ben Knight, Field Director, ERC." He was in charge of the Roboman fleet that had arrived in Muyang a couple of days ago to do the search and rescue. A man of indeterminate age, extremely fit, his shoulders almost as broad as the Roboman's. He wore a cap on his head that was more than simple wearing apparel; of metal and cloth, it was, laced through with electronics that allowed him to communicate with the Roboman. The Brain Interface Cap instantly translated his speech into machine language for the robot to understand.

The Roboman stepped aside, and Ben reached out to the girl. The girl, greatly relieved, did not hesitate to grasp his hand.

"My name is Ben," he said. "Bet you've never seen one of these robots before."

After a slight lag, to the girl's surprise, his speech was translated audibly into the local Thai language.

"It's okay." Ben continued. "You're safe now."

She shook her head, pointing to the Roboman, and muttering something so rapidly Ben's auto translator could not catch it fast enough. He really didn't care, though; this was not the time for soothing speeches.

"Look at me," Ben said gently but firmly, maintaining eye contact. "What is your name?"

"Tia."

"Tia," Ben replied. "You can't stay here, and I can't take you with me. This is a good machine that will take you to a safe place."

Cajoled rather than assured, she nodded. She willed herself to see something human in the Roboman, then closed her eyes, and yielded to her fate. Ben stepped aside; then the Roboman came forward again to lift her up and carry her away to a waiting trolley. It would return again to retrieve the body of the man.

At eight feet tall, these wide-chested robots were the pride of ERC. They were the most advanced humanoid robots created in the United States and the best offensive weapons for modern disaster search-and-rescue operations. Unlike the bulky Beasts of Burden built for manual labor and brute force, the Robomen moved with ease and scaled fluidly over obstacles. They moved faster than humans, learned quickly through experience and imitation, and were in constant communication with each other, always updating one another with what they'd learned—making the rescue mission a truly coordinated collaboration. It was this kind of communication that reduced redundancies in a disaster area where every nanosecond was a matter of life or death.

However, they had yet to comprehend complex emotions. When they were unable to pick up the finer cues of human reaction, a technician, usually working remotely, intervened and walked the Robot through the correct actions and speech. Ben could have easily controlled this rescue from his desk, giving the Roboman the words to say to calm the girl down, but he had always been a hands-on manager. He preferred to lead from the front, where he could react more quickly if a situation went unexpectedly wrong.

Ben breathed a sigh of relief as he watched the trolley carrying the girl head off to the safe zone. Dropped deep within the middle of the disaster zone, these transportation robots moved along self-assembling railroads, stopping to gather their human cargo, and creating veins through the disaster area. Once everyone was removed, the Beasts of Burden then came in to bulldoze the area, clearing it so that the community could start rebuilding as soon as possible. Even now, he could hear the grating sounds in the distance of the gigantic machines making inroads through the rubble, three-story metal pill-bugs the length and breadth of a small house. Like the trolleys, this new era of demolition equipment worked on their own, smart vehicles with the highest degree of autonomy, unlike the human-controlled trucks and cranes of the 2020s.

Satisfied with what he saw, Ben tapped the smartband strapped around his upper arm.

"We got the last one," he said. "The whole area is cleared. I'm heading back to the station for the countdown."

人

Across the globe, at the ERC Command Center, Henry Newman, the administrator for the company, watched the rescue mission from a 3-D image projected onto his table. He spoke directly to Ben's holoported image.

"I'm coming over for this one," Henry said.

Ben knew how to position his head to make it appear like his hologram was looking directly at Henry, which he did as he replied with a wry grin.

"Don't hurt yourself," Ben retorted.

Henry chuckled at Ben's teasing. Dressed immaculately, he had a full head of silver hair and a well-trimmed moustache, with a stance and commanding tone that revealed a military background. Though approaching retirement age, he was as sharp as a sea hawk and still as agile as the younger men and women who worked for him.

Henry had commanded hundreds of disaster rescues more than Ben but had to admit he was very impressed with how quickly Ben had handled this operation. It was only the third day, but they were well ahead of schedule and headed toward a new time record for the company, a fact which had the team abuzz with excitement.

⋏

Ben was not going to let himself rest even for a moment; every second mattered. He raced over to his car, the vehicle clicking into action as he approached, the engine already revved up by the time he leaped inside. As soon as he closed the hatch, the car did a short run and lifted off toward the horizon.

Looking over the city as he flew, Ben marveled at the extent of the damage. No matter how many times he had seen the results of an earthquake, he was always awed by its destructive power. He'd never gotten used to the sight of human suffering, could not shake the sadness that now enveloped him. Each disaster hit the same painful nerve, and each time he had to mentally block it out in order to continue his work. His mission was to rescue people, and there was no place for emotions.

But this was also a business, about who rescued the most humans in the least amount of time.

"The current record to clear a disaster area of live human beings is down to seventy-five hours," he said to himself, "set last month by the Chinese, and now everyone's racing to catch up…"

He cast a grim look out over the sight passing by below before continuing.

"…that record's about to be shattered."

CHAPTER 2

At the field station, Ben scanned the images of graphs and charts that displayed real-time data on the walls and checked the analysis and predictions of the inevitable setbacks before heading toward an olive-skinned woman seated behind several virtual screens. She had every appearance of being a serious nerd except for the beautiful dark movie star curls that fell perfectly around her head.

"The aftershock is still on target," she said. "Ten minutes."

Taylor Lovelace was just a few years out of college but was already a technical lead at ERC. Ambitious, she was wicked smart and condescendingly confident. She had received her first degree in geotechnical engineering when she was seventeen and went on to specialize in earthquake hazards on a fast track to obtain her doctorate. An incessant researcher, she had written many papers on disaster science, and her work was producing dividends for the company. It was no wonder that she was respected throughout the scientific community.

"Ten minutes is plenty of time for us to get ready for the countdown," Ben told her.

He was looking forward to officially closing this rescue mission as he meticulously went down his list, mentally checking off each item in order not to miss any detail, the most important of which was to check on the Robomen.

"Are the Robomen about done, Andre?" Ben asked as he turned to the young man sitting at the station next to Taylor's. He already knew the answer, though, just waited for the confirmation.

Andre Polokov was close to Taylor in age, but that was where the similarities ended. He looked like a perpetual university freshman. His clothes were shabby, and he smelled of the greasy takeout food that was his constant staple. Brilliant but lazy, he took the easy way at every opportunity he got. An avid gamer, Andre never took off his Brain Interface Cap, literally moving from his work to his games and then back to his work. It was hard for him to separate real life from the virtual, and it didn't surprise his coworkers that he understood the Robomen better than anyone.

On Andre's screen, the moon glistened off the rows of majestically silent Robomen lined up in a field not far from the station.

"The final group is on its way back to the loading area to join the rest and will be in hibernation shortly," Andre replied. "Shouldn't take five minutes."

"One more sweep just to be sure," Ben told him. "I know all the casualties have been removed, but I don't want to explain any surprises to Henry. Today's record is too important."

Andre wanted to protest, but he knew it was useless to try to change Ben's mind when he was so focused on a goal. Sighing, he started the field scanning program again. While the program was running, he worked on retrieving the infrastructure data of the town.

"All commercial data is extracted," he muttered after a moment, "but some of the residential data is missing."

"We need that residential data," Ben told him. "We need to compare it with other public records to make sure the rightful owners get their property back. Stolen disaster real estate has created a modern gold rush for thieves."

In truth, a skillful hacker from the comfort of his mother's basement could troll these calamities, erase or alter the information of the original owner, and sell the property off to a company within hours of a disaster. That company could claim ownership from anywhere in the world, and the global legal courts did not have enough resources to undo the damage. It would take years for some owners to claim back their property, if at all. However, after a number of very public property disputes turned deadly, many governments had set up a global initiative to map the infrastructure of each city as a backup. Big cities with a population of five million or more were required to store their real-estate information, not only in the cloud but also in miniservers that acted as a city's black box. Poorer nations, though, suffered the brunt of this thievery due to their inferior equipment and insufficient record-keeping.

"No need to worry," he called back as he worked, "I pride myself in beating the hackers at their game. I can still only work with what is available to me, though. Residential information was not properly recorded; about fourteen percent of it is missing."

Meanwhile, Taylor focused on the aftershock. Overlaying one power map over another on her virtual screen, she created a three-dimensional model to help her see how big it would be.

"I have the model up," she announced as she worked. "The area's already had several small aftershocks in the last few hours, but this one's different. It looks like it's gathering strength."

"Not good," Ben said with a shake of his head. "That could and cause additional loss of life and we would lose precious time."

"I'm not through with it yet," she promised, eyes fixed on her screen. "Don't forget—I'm the one who *created* all these industry-standard data-visualization tools. I'm using the data from the tremor vibrations to get ahead of this aftershock and predict its behavior."

"How long?" Ben asked.

"Even with the best tech," she replied, fingers flying across her keyboard, "still took about a couple of hours to gather enough data and render it for an accurate prediction. I used a little intuition based on current data as to where's a safe place to move the people to."

"Taylor, I trust your intuition better than most experts. You get better every time."

"Just as I predicted," she said with satisfaction, program code now scrolling by in one of her virtual screens, "the south is the best place for the temporary shelters. As it turned out, the final prediction came up with a definite indication that the tremors would strike to the north. I'm reworking the algorithm to improve workload distribution next time and thereby reduce rendering time."

⋏

The trolleys carrying the last group of survivors rolled into the safe zone. The compound was the length of two football fields and was now a fully functioning self-sufficient ecosystem. A dozen large buildings shaped like honeycombs, each honeycomb consisting of several bamboo hexagon-shaped cell houses that were rapidly assembled, were then stacked in rows one on top of the other. This shape allowed each house to get maximum light and privacy while taking up minimum space and also let each be fully insulated and solar powered. Due to their adaptability, they were increasingly used in all kinds of disasters. More durable than tents, they could be unstacked and reconfigured into permanent tiny houses for families, a better solution for the rapid rebuilding of a community and economy.

Vital in the first few days of disaster response were the two algae-generating tanks located at opposite corners of the camp. They prevented pollution by generating oxygen, helped clear the air around the cell houses, and also produced an energy-and-food source in the dire conditions of the first few days of the rescue operation, when aid trucks are prohibited from entering until the second stage.

The wounded were carried out first and into the caring hands of human medic teams, those with the most life-threatening injuries being airlifted to the nearest emergency medical centers. The healthy and those with minor injuries, including Tia, the girl Ben had rescued, were bused to the temporary housing, where Tia's eyes widened when she saw the bright warm room she would share with other women.

She was handed a sleeping bag, a bottle of water, and algae food packets by a service robot and then sat enraptured as a virtual assistant played soothing songs to her that she remembered from her youth to put her at ease. She wasn't scared of the machines anymore, and so she settled in a corner to lay her bruised body on the bedding and was asleep before the other women could introduce themselves.

Chapter 3

Andre couldn't believe his ears. The scanning program had picked up a heat source, and it was confirmed by an alarm going off.

"You missed someone," Ben told him.

"I swear I cleared the entire area," he replied. "I checked the dilapidated building earlier, and there were no humans. I'm running the scanning program over the area again."

Pulling up a map of the city, he zeroed in on the location of the distress signal.

"Got it," he said a moment later. "Infrared puts it right on top of a slab in that same building. Don't know how I missed that."

"I want that record, people," Ben stated, looking anxiously at the clock. "We're breaking that seventy-five-hour mark."

"I'm using the x-ray vision and laser to build an image of what's underneath that slab," Taylor said as she worked quickly at her terminal. "About... twenty feet under. Looks like the body of a woman, but no movement. Going deeper with the mics."

She turned up the volume, and for a moment, all was quiet and tense in the room. Then through the speakers came the distinctive sound of a heartbeat.

"Actually, you missed two," Taylor said, throwing Andre an accusing look. "Hear that? It's a baby, and it's alive. I can't tell if it is outside her body or inside, though."

"One Roboman will do," Ben said with a tight voice. "Medics should head to the location."

On his screen, Andre quickly selected a Roboman; it took off running.

"Go get them, Slade," he said.

"Slade? You gave it a name?" Taylor asked.

"Robot model S-878 doesn't roll off the tongue that easily," Andre replied with a grin.

"You know it's just a machine, don't you?"

"Don't mind her, Slade," he said, addressing his screen. "She didn't mean it."

⋏

The Roboman Slade scaled the building, jumping down, and landing softly next to the slab and then tossed the multiton slab aside like a rag doll to reveal the dead woman curled protectively over a screaming baby. Slade picked up the baby, made its way to the top of the building, and handed it to the medics.

It then returned, picked up the dead woman, and scrambled up again, scanning the dead woman's palm with a laser before placing the body on a gurney. Soon the gurney was in a trolley moving away for the area. The whole sequence took a matter of minutes, but Ben was frustrated. There was the risk of the aftershock, and the countdown was in jeopardy.

"This is not acceptable." Ben said through clenched teeth.

"Hey," Taylor said, "we saved a baby."

Ben willed himself to calm down. Taylor was right, as always, but mistakes were costly. Henry would be materializing in hologram form at any moment, and he would need an explanation.

A short time later, Henry's hologram appeared on Ben's desk...just in time for the echo of screams to come piercing through from several of the monitors. The trolley with the rescued baby had just arrived at the camp, but suddenly Slade began destroying everything in his path. Terrified people were fleeing before a swirling cloud of dust.

"What's wrong?" said Henry.

"Andre," Ben snapped.

"I'm not sure what happened to Slade," Andre replied in a panic. "His functions are way off. He's out of control."

"It's deviated from its initial design," Taylor said as she drilled down on the robot's status. "But I don't see any transitional anomalies."

"Slade, return to Search and Rescue...I repeat, return to Search and Rescue."

Ignoring Andre's command, the Roboman yanked hard at the empty trolley and lifted it up. As it swung the car over its head, part of its right pinky got caught and tore off.

Andre desperately pounded his keyboard, entering different commands with no success.

"Override its policy function," Taylor suggested.

"He's not responding," Andre reported. "Sensors are down."

"Wipe it then," Taylor snapped. "Revert to initial state."

Ben had had enough. "We don't have time. Switch it to manual, *now.*"

"Manual?" Taylor said. "Ben, you're not going out there! I can execute a fail-safe from here."

"You'll do nothing of the sort," Ben said. "I'm not going to lose a Roboman without first trying to get it under control. They're just too expensive; destruction is a *last* resort. The paperwork and explanations I'd have to make to the financiers would be a nightmare."

He put on his Brain Interface Cap, grabbed a minitablet, and touched a panel in the wall that slid away to reveal a safe. He then placed his palm on a red pad next to the safe's door; it changed to a blinking yellow.

"Henry?" Ben said.

Henry's hologram did the same with a pad before his own desk. The pad by the safe door turned green, and the door snapped open, revealing a stash of laser injectors. One of these injectors could incapacitate a robot, and when necessary, destroy the machine. Ben grabbed an injector and made his way to the door.

"Please don't get hurt," Taylor whispered after him.

"Relax," Andre told her, "he can take care of himself. What you should worry about is whether he'll zap the Roboman or risk his neck to try and save it."

"Dude," Taylor snarled, "your sense of humor stinks!"

⚰

Ben jumped out of his car before it came to a stop and sprinted toward the buildings, concealing his approach in the shadows. He snuck up behind Slade and slid to the ground and then quickly entered a series of commands into the minitablet. The information seemed to take a lifetime to load.

"Come on!" he growled in frustration under his breath.

When the commands finally loaded on his computer, Ben breathed a sigh of relief and then pressed the Execute button. His Brain Interface Cap beeped, acknowledging the information was received. Slade instantly picked up the familiar sound and turned, spotting Ben immediately.

Ben knew he was in trouble. He had barely released the safety on the laser injector, when the Roboman was upon him. From the corner of his eye, he saw the metallic hand snake out and grab his neck. His head exploded with pain, and his arms went momentarily limp, his pen dropping and rolling away out of reach. Ben tried desperately to twist away, kicking at the Robot's legs to distract it. He strained toward the tablet, his fingers clawing at the tiny keyboard pad until he could jab at the Execute key once again. The command finally came through, and Slade froze.

"There, there. Easy," Ben said as he pried himself from the steel grip.

Wheezing, he groped around for the pen until he found it and put the safety carefully back on. He then looked at his watch. A loud drone filled the air; it was the aftershock. He heard Henry shout in his earpiece.

"Brace yourself!"

The earth gave way beneath Ben and Slade. Ben desperately reached up, but there was nothing to hold on to as he slid into the darkness, followed quickly by Slade.

⚰

When the shaking finally stopped, Taylor jumped back into her seat to set some camera drones speeding out for the last place Ben had been seen, desperately trying to find any sign of him in the rubble. She hadn't been searching that long, when she saw movement at the edge of the hole. To her relief, Ben's hand appeared and gripped the top of the hole as he pulled himself up and out of danger.

The room erupted in elation.

"That was way too close," Taylor said.

"Time for the countdown," Henry's hologram said.

Taylor scrambled to check the safe zones to see if her predictions held true.

"No additional loss of life," she exclaimed with relief.

Above her report, the Logistics Robot continued the countdown. Another cheer went up as they all screamed out "zero."

"Seventy-two hours," Andre called out. "A record!"

"Commence second phase," the Logistics Robot announced.

"Well done, Ben," Henry's voice said in his ear as he started back. "We have ourselves a new world record."

As dawn washed over the skyline of Muyang, the Beasts of Burden drove systematically through the rough terrain, breaking down concrete walls and tarmac pieces into smaller bits. Behind them, the bulldozers followed chomping the broken pieces into powder and pushing the pulverized material into neat blocks. The city was on its way to rebuilding.

⋏

Three days of nonstop intense work had finally taken its toll. Taylor sat upright in her chair, dead asleep. Slumped over his desk, Andre snored loudly. From another desk, Henry's hologram held up a glass of champagne to Ben as he in turn poured himself a drink and took a gulp.

"You look like death warmed over," Henry quipped.

"Thanks." Ben grinned. "And here I thought no one would notice."

"You know what this means," Henry stated, barely able to contain his excitement.

"Not so fast," Ben told him. "We've brought down the error rate, but we need more robot speed. The machine code could use a thorough update."

"The code's fine," Henry replied. "We should just avoid mistakes like today's."

"Trust me," Ben said, "that won't happen again."

"It better not. We can't afford a setback. The investors are fickle enough as it is."

As Henry's image disappeared in a wink, Ben knew that what he'd said was true. Like any other company that relied on investors, they not only faced long hours and conflicts with family but also had to worry constantly about fund-raising. He drained his drink as he felt the tiredness overtake him.

He glanced briefly over to the sleeping forms of Andre and Taylor; then with a tired smile, he raised a silent toast to them before setting down his glass with a yawn and a stretch.

"I have to find out what caused the malfunction that almost derailed everything," he said, as he sat back. "I'm convinced it was a vulnerability in the code that caused Slade to react like that, but it could be anything. I'll check the known bugs first, but if there's nothing there, then I'll have to create new code for unknown scenarios, and I'm not looking forward to it."

"Uh, what did you say?" Taylor asked, talking in her sleep.

Ben laughed as her head dropped down again.

"First, I'll have to make a stop at the server center in Iceland on my way home. Make sure no memory transferred from Slade via neural networks going back into the memory cells; we don't need this happening again somewhere else. I'll check every cell and network myself if I have to," he said, sighing wearily. "I'm not looking forward to telling Mindy about another delay in getting home."

Chapter 4

Even with all the autonomous appliances available and the robo-chefs taking over the kitchens of middle-class households, Mindy Knight preferred to prepare meals for her family the old-fashioned way: with her own hands.

"Breakfast is ready," she shouted.

Mindy had always wanted to have a family, and when she married Ben, she willingly gave up her career to stay home with her children. The first two, Ashlynn and Chase, arrived on schedule, completing her picture of a perfect family. Then JR came along; he was a total surprise. Not only had they not planned for him he came with a bagful of medical challenges that kept them hospital-bound most of his early life. Eventually, Ben returned to full-time work at ERC that required him to travel all over the globe, and as he took on more operational roles, he was gone for longer periods. Eight years later, she was resigned to his frequent absences. Her features echoed the weight she felt of bringing up the children mostly on her own. She knew he was trying hard and took every opportunity he got to be with them, but it still was not enough time. Today he was kind of present, holoported into his seat at the dining table. She forced herself to smile as she set the food on the table and began to prepare JR's supplements.

"Sorry, you can't have any of this," she teased.

Ben's hologram was real enough for her to reach out and touch him, yet she could not bring herself to do it. His attention was elsewhere, and she could tell by his gestures and eye movement that he was working.

"When did you say you would be home?" she asked.

"I'll be on the next flight," he replied.

JR came down bouncing down the stairs followed by Max, the family dog.

"Dad!" JR called out. "I got a new game, but Chase won't play with me."

"We'll play together when I get home."

"Can you play with me now? I've sent it to you already."

Mindy and Ben looked at each other. They knew he wasn't going to let go of that idea any time soon.

"Hey, before you start having fun, young man," Mindy stated, "you must take your supplements."

Mindy measured the portions of his cocktail breakfast of organic juices and supplements, counted out the approved pills, then lined them up in the order she would administer them to JR.

"Open up," Mindy insisted.

"But Mom—" JR protested.

Mindy dropped the first pill down JR's throat and had him take a sip of water before he had time to close his mouth.

"Yuck! But Mom," JR continued, in between gulps, "why won't Chase play with me?"

"Chase has to go to work," Ben told him.

"Play with me, Dad," JR insisted.

"Tomorrow, JR," Ben replied.

JR was part of a growing population of children who were on a supervised federal medical program and monitored constantly by the hospitals. Due to the disastrous aftereffects of overmedicating children in the past decades during the opioid epidemic that turned many into pill-dependent adults, the current programs leaned heavily on counseling, providing organic solutions and stimulation to help the children become better-functioning adults rather than drug-addicted zombies.

JR sneezed, drawing an anxious look from Mindy.

"You let Max sleep on your bed again?" Mindy asked.

Max's ears perked when he heard his name, eyes pleading.

"Mom, Max is my best friend," JR insisted.

"And your biggest allergen," she reminded him. "I have too much to deal with as it is until your father gets back, so I'm afraid that Max will just have to go off to the sitter for a bit."

"Ah, Mom…"

Ashlynn and Chase walked into the dining room together. Chase was a lanky seventeen-year-old, who towered over his mother as he bent to give her a kiss and a hug, then sat down, and wolfed down his food without acknowledging his dad. Ashlynn's face lit up with a smile when she saw her father's hologram, but it quickly changed to a pout. She planted herself directly in front of Ben's image.

"Where are you, Dad?" she asked. "You're gonna miss my first game."

At nineteen years old, Ashlynn was a beauty, and she knew it. Ben melted instantly. He could never resist her charms for long.

"I'm in Iceland, honey, and I'll be on the first flight out as soon as I've checked out things here."

"You always say that," Ashlynn said. "Doesn't he, Chase?"

Chase did not respond. He missed his dad, but he wasn't going to let him see that vulnerable side of him. He compensated for the void by being irritatingly protective of his mother. It was easier to disengage than to try to strike up a conversation that would only make him angrier.

Chase's phone rang.

"Don't answer it," Ben told him. "This is family time."

"It's Grandpa Jessie; he's family," Chase retorted. He pushed back his chair and walked away, while JR still hoped to engage his dad in his game. He inched closer to the virtual disc on the floor by Ben's hologram, intrigued by a blinking red dot reflecting off Ben's hologram.

"Dad, fight me."

JR held up his phone to show his dad the start of the game.

"I can't right now. What's the name of the game?"

"Never mind," JR said and sighed, very much disappointed.

"Come on, buddy," Ben told him. "Tomorrow, promise."

JR shrugged his shoulders and put his phone away.

Chase said good-bye to his Grandpa, loud enough for everyone to hear him, and then returned to the table to finish his breakfast. JR, though, was still angry and wanted to get Chase in trouble.

"Did you know that Chase is going to fly with Grandpa?"

"Well," Chase replied, "I'd go flying with Dad, but he's away saving the world."

Mindy was appalled. "Chase!"

Ben frowned.

Chase snatched JR's phone from him and pulled his ear, setting off a shoving contest.

"It's a stupid game."

"It isn't," JR protested. "Why won't you play with me?"

"Coz, it serves you right, tattle-tale." The boys went at it, the older egging on the increasingly frustrated younger one, before JR went into a sneezing fit.

"Cut it out, boys," Mindy shouted. "Chase, you are going to make your brother sick."

"Stop it guys," Ben said. "Okay, JR I'll play with you."

JR's bout of sneezing came to a rapid end.

"Now?"

"Yes, but only for five minutes."

Mindy let out a sigh of relief.

Of late, Mindy couldn't fight off the doubts that kept nudging her. She had met Ben almost twenty years ago, yet she still knew so little about her husband. Drawn to his magnetic personality and charm, she had instantly fallen in love with him, and when he asked her to marry him four weeks later, she didn't hesitate to say yes. It didn't matter that he didn't talk much about his past at first—only that he had been married before and recently become a widower. She knew his first wife had died after a short illness, and his son soon afterward. Obviously, it hurt him to talk about it, and Mindy was not one to probe. Eventually, he opened up to her enough to fill in some of the gaps. It helped that his dad visited regularly and told the children all sorts of stories about Ben's childhood.

The first years were bliss. He was an attentive husband and a doting father, who fiercely loved his children. Many times, she would find him asleep holding a child as if he never wanted to let go. Then Henry and ERC came calling. Ben took to the company like a man possessed. Gradually, ERC took over his life until Mindy could not remember the man she had fallen in love with. When he came home, he was always very apologetic and tried to give the children his whole attention. It never lasted long, though. A few days later, the company would call, and he would once again be gone. Yet once in a while, Ben would surprise her with flowers and a longer visit.

But they were becoming just that; visits.

⅄

Ben walked down the hallway of the neat rows of servers followed by a nervous group of engineers. The place was quiet except for the constant hum of refrigeration as it cooled down the hub of the cryogenic memory cells. He had driven the technicians hard to meticulously test every area for any lingering memory of the misbehavior and erase it. Every connection and node was retested, but he needed them to do it one more time.

"We've tested every cell, sir," one of the engineers said.

"Do it again," Ben insisted.

"But, sir, they're all clean."

"You heard me. I expect a report before I land in Chicago," Ben replied as he left the room.

He stepped out into a winter wonderland. The ERC datacenter was just outside Reykjavik, Iceland. A cold wind was bringing in an early snowstorm and adding to the inches already on the ground. He wanted to get out of there as soon as possible and not have to explain another delay to Mindy, when he had promised her he would be at the game.

CHAPTER 5

Wolf Nelson, the president of the United States, walked briskly down the hallway from the Oval Office, surrounded by the usual presidential entourage. As the first Native American president in office, he was the perfect cultured product of a political system determined to increase the recent diversity trend in the government all the way up to the top. His youth and handsome features had made him popular with all voters, especially the young adults. He, in turn, promised he would stay engaged with them throughout his term in office. Each morning he rose early to play virtual games with any challenger who dared him, to the extent that his gamer achievements were more hotly debated in social media than his political agenda, a strategy that helped keep his poll numbers up and silence his political rivals.

Darci Woods, the president's communications director, hurried to catch up with the group. She was a no-nonsense woman, elegant, and with impeccable style; highly respected, if not feared, in the inner circles of the political arena. Over the years, Darci had become a close confidante to President Nelson and influenced many of the decisions he made. She was not afraid to give him her honest opinion, and Wolf respected that. When offered the position, she had not refused his offer; it was ambiguous enough for her to be broad in the interpretation of her work.

"The security level is still red, so today's briefing is remote," Darci's aide whispered in her ear to bring her up to speed.

Darci nodded.

Wolf gave her a quick nod of recognition, "What's up with Europe this morning?"

"And a good morning to you, too, Mr. President," Darci answered.

"Come on Darci," he said, "something's bothering you. You're never late."

"It's just that this was never an issue. Why is this happening now?" Darci spoke like she moved, with great precision, something that transferred from her previous life as a CIA operative.

"I'm still in the dark," the president reminded her.

They entered the press briefing room; it was empty except for a podium. Darci pointed her phone to a wall, and Wolf's image materialized on the flat surface. He was speaking before a large group of booing delegates.

"The EU delegates got vicious yesterday. They'll try to destroy your confidence again."

"What almost destroyed me yesterday was I got hacked," President Nelson stated.

Darci ignored the whining.

The president stepped behind the podium, and immediately his aides swarmed him. His face received a touch of makeup, his hair was brushed, and the microphones were repositioned. A miniature virtual teleprompter was at Wolf's eye level. Lines began to roll.

"Remember, keep your answers short," Darci told him. "That will discourage any journalist's rush of enthusiasm to pick on the irrelevant stuff. Keep in mind, the earthquake rescue effort will occupy the lion's share of the questions."

But the president was not about to let his grievance be swept away so easily. "All it took was one word out of place," he reminded her, "which you allowed."

Dwight Ellison, the Secretary of State, heard the president's complaints as he walked in and could not resist a dig.

"Seriously, Darci, you have to keep those hackers out of the president's private cloud," he said. "You can't keep making him a victim of delivering fake news."

"Do you have any idea," she scowled back at Dwight, "how many people work tirelessly every second to stop those idiots?"

"Well, one got in, and I find that quite intriguing," he replied. "Do something about it, won't you? Makes us look juvenile."

"Yeah, and I'm just eating bonbons," Darci retorted.

"Don't act so naïve," Dwight hissed. "I bet, you know whodunit. Don't you, Sherlock?"

It was obvious there was no love lost between the two of them. Dwight was a slick lizard with an artificial tan and a plastic smile. Deceitful and reckless, he saw himself as the man who protected the interests of the president as long as he benefited from them. It was easy for him to justify betraying anyone and even his country. In turn, Dwight had long suspected Darci of protecting a sub-rosa intelligence organization that kept her well informed of what was going on around the world. These were people she had worked with in her past, but he was convinced many of them were hardened criminals. He was always on the lookout for information about her, which he could use against her if she ever tried to blackmail him.

"You heard the rescue operation in Asia was successful?" Darci said, ignoring his jab.

"Ah, anything to change the subject," Dwight said. "That robot fleet that you defend so faithfully is old. The machine code has plateaued, and from what I hear, is highly unstable."

"We set a record," Darci replied. "That's what matters. Every person who was still alive was rescued within seventy-two hours and before a big aftershock hit. That fleet will be doing business for the United States for a long time."

"Standby," an aide interrupted.

The aide held up her hand, signaling the final countdown was about to begin. Darci and Dwight moved away from the president.

"But what do we get in return?" President Nelson asked.

"At the moment? Hope," Darci said defensively.

"Come on, that's not a fair exchange of goods, is it?" he protested.

"The important thing is the world knows we are still a superpower," Darci said.

The image on the wall changed to a duplicate image of the present setup with President Nelson speaking in a prerecorded session.

"Disaster response is a money pit squeezing the life out of us," Dwight stated.

"It supports American businesses," Darci retorted.

"Point taken, but there's the budget to consider," the president interrupted them. "At the end of the day, Darci, Muyang is just another government-sponsored field test."

"Sounds like a veto to me," Dwight said, his grin showing how much he was enjoying this. "Let's hope we see an increase in the disaster commodity index soon."

"Five…Four…" The aide started the countdown, silently mouthing down the last three seconds, and then pointed to the president. Multiple journalists sitting in a remote press room holoported into the room, several raising their hands immediately.

"Yes, Bill," Wolf began. "You have a question about the rescue effort?"

"Yes, Mr. President," one of the journalists replied. "Ever since the great earthquake in California two years ago, the financial burden of recovery has crippled the US economy. Why do we continue to pour taxpayer money elsewhere, when we have a such terrible need here?"

"I know you've read up on this, Bill, but ignoring global disasters like the one in Muyang, Thailand, can only be to our detriment," the president replied. "Getting these affected areas back up and running not only saves lives, which is the humane thing to do, but it saves the US money in the long run by getting those economies functioning again as soon as possible. We now know one single sizable disaster anywhere in the world sets off ripples that cause global economic degradation. It isn't like fifty years ago, when an Ebola epidemic in West Africa or a tsunami in South Asia had little to no effect on the rest of the world as it does now. We've learned that ignoring these events make for very expensive mistakes."

President Nelson then turned to a bespectacled, statuesque blonde. Bly Cochrane's retro-2020s look was striking against the modern attire of the rest of the journalists, as was her height and beauty. She gained popularity during his campaign, when she mobilized the young adults, causing a shift that helped him win the presidency. She was also a good gamer, who challenged Wolf at his game regularly. She had become one of the most popular journalists and had a knack for catching him off guard with her quick-witted questions.

Wolf braced inwardly and hoped he had prepared enough for her laser questions.

"Yes, Bly."

"Rescue companies of the other nations name their price for these disaster response services; however, distressed nations are usually poor and lack hard cash, and the US takes payments-in-kind such as a hundred barrels of oil or a block of real estate. Isn't that robbery? There are global coalitions and bilateral agreements that would ensure developed countries like ours don't get too greedy. The watchdogs watch watchdogs."

"Great question, Bly," he replied. "We successfully eliminated the trillion-dollar deficit that plagued the country at the beginning of the twenty-first century. As you already know, this was done by the government working alongside private companies and by splitting profits, successfully pulled the nation out of its monetary rut. Many countries are not there yet, and certainly payments in kind are imperative for us to continue this very important work. It's our fair wages, and that isn't greed."

But she wasn't finished and jumped in again before he could turn to another journalist.

"With an aging fleet of Robomen," she asked, "how do we expect to get ahead of the bigger and newer fleets being developed in Europe and Asia?"

"We just set a world record with that same fleet. All lives were saved in sixty hours. They are keeping up with the competition," President Nelson said.

Bly hesitated and checked the notes on her pad.

"With all due respect sir, that sounds like an exaggeration. Did you mean seventy-two hours, sir?" she quizzed softly.

Wolf instinctively looked off to his side at Darci. The quick glance was not lost on the ever-revealing cameras. Was that a glimmer in Bly's eye? She had succeeded in rattling him again. The journalists, smelling juicy gossip, hurried to send out quick notes on the mistake that would be the talk for the next hour in social media. Darci hurriedly left the briefing room.

Out in the hallway, Darci paced as she spoke into her near-invisible mouthpiece.

"The president was fed a wrong line! Obviously, the malware escaped all your security checks, Pete," Darci said.

"Yes, ma'am," the security lead responded in her earpiece.

"Again!"

"Yes, ma'am."

"Fix it."

"Ma'am, this is new; it's a just-begun."

Darci couldn't hide her surprise. "A what?"

"Whoever's adjusting the text is doing it on the fly," Pete replied. "A minute ago, the world didn't have this code."

Darci froze in her tracks, her mind swiftly buzzing through the possibilities.

CHAPTER 6

The light of a disco ball cast eclectic shadows on a boisterous crowd egging on a group of hackers engaged in a virtual competition. A graph of digital piles of chips, projected on one wall of the room, tallied the competitors' progress, the global news scrolling across a banner above it. On the opposite wall was a vibrant digital painting titled "Onions Caressed by Silk Handkerchiefs." This was Room 25 on Sandwich, a private underground gambling room. Guests were allowed in by invitation only.

The dealer kept an eagle's eye on the one player well ahead of the pack. At first glance, Scott Adams was forgettable, but after a few minutes of watching him code, any thoughts of mediocrity were quickly erased. As the game progressed, the looks of curiosity by the first-time visitors changed to downright admiration. Scott's icy glares could not put off the envious looks of the other players ogling his growing pile of chips. This was not the first time Scott had been here and won in a big way. The dealer had long suspected he was cheating but had never proven it and knew better than to make a scene without evidence. That was for his bosses to figure out. Besides, the man brought in good business, counting by the number of fools who kept upping their bets and losing to him.

Scott's colorless demeanor was intentional. He was a chameleon, a true modern-day hacker. The son of two British spies, he was an expert at being invisible in plain sight, and he lied like he played, with fluidity. However, if his layers of confidence were pulled back, one would find they covered up the insecurity of a desperately lonely childhood that had been the inevitable result of his parents' chosen vocation. As an adult, he sought attention in the underground world to replace the void that his parents' love would have filled. He had become a legend in the hacking world. Nothing gave him a greater thrill than when he outsmarted the system.

"Two seconds," the dealer announced.

Scott typed rapidly and hit the *enter* key.

"And...he's done it again," exclaimed the dealer.

Cheers erupted from the crowd, which became louder when a news flash banner scrolled across the screen promising breaking news.

Scott was bored. He stretched and looked around, his gaze settling on a beautiful woman standing by the door, away from the crowd.

"I think I'll turn in early," Scott said.

Admirers groaned, but the competitors were relieved, exhausted both mentally and financially.

"Aren't you going to wait for the rest of the news, sir?" asked the dealer. "The night is still young in Vienna."

Scott looked pointedly at the dealer.

"Your winnings will be processed as usual, sir, in the cryptocurrency of your choice," the dealer said and sighed with resignation. "Have a good night, sir."

As Scott walked up toward the door, he brushed up against the woman. In a flash, he pick-pocketed her phone and slipped the device into his pocket. He had seen the woman come in earlier and sensed she hadn't come to enjoy the game but to watch him.

Once out in the deserted hallway, Scott inserted a flashcard into the stolen phone. "Let's find out who you really are."

Scott scanned the lines of code as they rushed by on the phone's screen. He didn't recognize the name "Kim Brown Okamoto" that materialized. Scott smiled at the challenge, but then a message popped up that wiped the smirk off his face.

"Scott, get out *now*, and I don't mean the hotel."

Scott quickly dismantled the phone and kicked the remains under a table; then he stepped out of the hotel into the darkness making sure he was not followed. Outside in the shadows, he sucked off the fake prints from his fingertips and swallowed them, before joining the unsuspecting evening strollers and fading into the crowd.

CHAPTER 7

It was a beautiful September day in Haywood, Kansas. The Indian summer warmth washed over the comfortably spaced picturesque houses with immaculate green lawns against the backdrop of gentle rolling hills. Families walked their dogs and pushed strollers along tree-lined pavements, as delightful laughter floated from the town's playground.

The pristine beauty was interrupted by a large, modern building in the middle of town. The architect had designed it to be a seamless integration with its surroundings, merging with the landscape. Its ivy-covered terraces were a great display of environmental sensitivity, but the sheer size of its steel framework and concrete walls made it a sore sight. This was the central headquarters of ERC; its location was deliberately chosen because Haywood had one unique trait: it was the safest place in the nation. This claim was backed by three decades of statistics that showed no serious natural disasters had occurred in the area in almost thirty years, and predictive analysis showed no change from that trend in the near future.

The massive open working area inside the ERC headquarters was surprisingly warm and comfortable. Several technicians stood or sat at stations in front of virtual workspaces. Everything was set up to reduce fatigue on the human body. The space was designed to ensure natural light came into the darkest corners, and the temperature was regulated perfectly; even the air was circulated and fully refreshed every hour to reduce the risk of airborne diseases. Personal assistants and service robots were numerous, assisting with the mundane activities.

Technicians moved around freely because they were not tied to a physical desk and could set up their virtual workspace virtually anywhere and project work onto any surface—a wall, a table, even the palm of a hand—freeing them up to move and change positions without breaking their workflow. Like many workers in this new global economy, these techs worked around the clock in shifts as the machines compiled, rendered, and analyzed earthquake data from all around the globe.

The workers donned wearable devices in or on their clothing. Many preferred to wear their communication devices on their upper arms or shoulders, where they were easy to activate by voice, touch, or gesture. Everything was connected by wireless microphones, cameras, and sensors that captured sound and movement.

The group that worked directly with the Robomen in the field wore the Brain Interface Caps like Ben. These technicians provided backup for the field, allowing ERC to communicate with or control the robots in an emergency. With a quick tilt or flick of the hand, a tech could adjust the direction of a Beast of Burden or overrule a Roboman's action halfway across the world. This control was especially important in compromised situations when the robot could not arrive at a viable conclusion to save a human being, and backup from the center could make the difference between life and death.

Taylor and Andre, back from their recent assignment, studied the world map displayed on Taylor's screen, looking for signs of increasing earthquake activity. Andre's gaze, however, was fixed on the delicate features of Taylor's face. He could not help admiring how beautiful she looked in the soft light reflected on the screen.

With a graceful flick of her hand, Taylor zoomed in on Chicago and pulled up several analysis tables that showed detailed waves of Earth's movements. She turned the area on a pivot stopping at Lake Michigan.

"Look at this tremor pattern around Lake Michigan."

She moved her pointer to bring the area into more detail with higher resolution and added a pattern analysis on top of it. Andre hesitantly turned his head and studied the images and charts.

"Strange," he noted, "I've never seen that kind of activity around Chicago. What do you think?"

"There's not enough data to predict anything yet," Taylor replied. "Chicago has no big active faults, but there's always a first time. Maybe the New Madrid fault line's getting a little restless. I think the tremors will increase, but there's nothing that threatening to warrant a call in."

Andre shrugged and clicked through a few screens, searching carefully. "They are not increasing much…no peaks. The tremors around Singapore are more powerful."

Andre turned the globe to show Singapore. There was clearly more activity there. Taylor sighed.

"I guess we're heading back to Asia."

Andre's eyes lit up. "You do get tired of these things!"

Taylor was confused by his earnest enthusiasm.

"No, not really. Just weary of traveling, but that doesn't last. We have to learn as much as possible, and every quake is essential for us saving lives, more lives."

Andre was surprised by her passion and quickly changed the subject.

"I'm not looking forward to you regurgitating your technical reports on the plane," he told her.

"Why not? It's good for your brain. Can't wait to tell you about the latest trends in electrical resistivity tomography."

Andre made a face. "I would rather chug down raw fish brains on a bed of warm liver pate."

He smiled to himself; secretly, he looked forward to their debates.

⅄

Scott, wearing dark glasses, was the last to get on the plane. Much to the surprise of the customer-service girl at the gate, there had been a last-minute cancelation on the standby list, and a seat had become available for him, to which Scott now made his way.

Ben Knight was sprawled across it, fast asleep.

"Excuse me," Scott said to him.

Ben pulled himself up, shaking off the mental cobwebs, and then Scott slid past him and sat quickly down.

"Ladies and gentlemen," the attendant announced, "we'll be on our way to Chicago shortly."

Chapter 8

The slick and modern skyscrapers made of the latest disaster-proof and environment-friendly materials stood in stark contrast to the older architecture of brick and mortar in the Chicago skyline. Digital billboards created an ever-changing kaleidoscope of advertisement downtown, among which a heavily promoted comeback tour of Brandon Bosk, a wildly successful teenage pop star at the beginning of the century, looped every few moments on several screens.

In the streets, aerodynamic electric cars with vibrant colors and personalized designs mingled with the automatic hybrid cars preferred by the older generation. A solid population of multiwheeled scooters and bicycles had their own pathways and lights paralleling the car traffic, while above it all messenger drones flew in their own orderly aerial byways. In the suburbs, flying cars landed and taxied to the end of various cul-de-sacs. They had become the preferred mode of transportation of the upper middle class, who were now used to getting door-to-door service. These were also popular among mobile nurses and technical handymen catering to an aging millennial population.

The newer homes in the suburbs were smaller in comparison to the mansions of yesterday. They were made with a blend of bamboo, flex glass, and carbon-reinforced plastic materials with rubber and steel cables. Judging by the number of recycling bins in each compound, it seemed like everything was recycled, and compost pits were a required addition to every backyard.

This modern world came with a new set of laws and regulations trying to slow down the exponential progression of global warming, which had been predicted by analyst prophets of the yesteryears and was now a living reality. Rationing and intentional recycling in every part of life had become an everyday occurrence at all levels of community. There were government-monitored health requirements with strict mandates on diet and exercise regimens that brought down the cost of public health care, which had skyrocketed at the beginning of the millennium. It had finally leveled off considerably to the extent the entire population had affordable medical coverage. More people took the time to exercise outdoors, and today was no exception.

The parks were filled with crowds looking for fun in the afternoon sun. Babies cooed, teenagers kissed, mothers gossiped, even the police officers cracked a smile or two. A couple laughed at their baby's surprised expression when she saw her contorted image reflected in the giant, stainless steel Bean sculpture.

At the Chicago mall, middle-aged women dressed in blue vintage attire waited impatiently outside the arena for the doors to open. Once inside the lit room, the digital images of a middle-aged Brandon Bosk beamed from the walls. His biggest hits blared from speakers around the room as the women rushed to the stage to secure their positions. Granted they would have to listen to the opening act before he appeared, but they were unable to contain their excitement and raced to the empty stage, vying to get as close as possible. These fans followed Bosk wherever he performed, keeping him in business. They reminisced about the old days on social media, bought all his promotional materials, and paid a pretty penny for the VIP backstage tickets. Likewise, Bosk who had endured much ridicule over the years, showed his deep appreciation for them by belting out the oldies with genuine gusto and gratitude, taking all the time in the world to pose with them and listen to their family stories.

"I can't wait to give him a big old sloppy kiss when I see him," one awestruck fan exclaimed above the noise.

Not everyone was in Chicago for Brandon Bosk, however. The baseball season had been good to the Cubs, and after a long drought, they were well on their way to reaching the postseason again. Excitement built up among the crowd as the baseball players prepared for the opening pitch. There was no open seat in the Wrigley Stadium.

Chase walked between the bleachers, selling hotdogs from the box he carried. He liked this job because he got paid while he watched the game. He was saving up for a faster hoverboard.

"One hotdog," shouted a customer from the bleachers.

"Coming right up," Chase replied.

Chase put the order into a fingerprint reader and held it out to the customer who pressed his index finger on it. The gadget bleeped for a second, and a digital receipt completed the transaction, spewing out the payment information.

"Fifteen dollars," Chase said as he handed him the food. "Safe for you to eat, Mr. A. J. Brown. It contains no nuts or shellfish."

Mindy stood outside the family suite, chatting with a group of friends, occasionally leaning over to check on JR, who was inside the suite. As usual, he was oblivious to the world, playing games on his phone with Max cuddled next to him. She had time to grab another coffee before the game began and so headed to the beverage stand.

Ashlynn stood on a small makeshift platform next to the home plate on the baseball field. She looked elegant in her red dress with a blue and white scarf, but had never felt so nervous in her life. She licked her dry lips and did some quick trills to warm up her voice. Though it was steady, she could not keep her hands from trembling. Tom, the cameraman, noticed her discomfort.

"Hey, singing the national anthem at the biggest game of the season is just a walk in the park," he teased.

The pun did not draw the expected laughter.

She again nervously licked her lips. Out of the corner of her eye, Ashlynn noticed a rat scurrying past her feet. Startled but too surprised to scream, she looked curiously after it, then at Tom as both of them began to sway. A slow, anguished drone that sounded like a freight train filled the air. Vibrations shimmered through Ashlynn, but she was too immobilized by fear to move. The ground was shifting underneath her.

"Earthquake!" Tom shouted.

Terrified, he dropped his equipment and fled. He was halfway across the field, when the earth opened up, and he disappeared into the darkness. Ashlynn screamed, stumbled backward, but steadied herself and ran in the opposite direction.

In the bleachers, people bumped and toppled over each other as they rushed toward the exit tunnels, the stronger elbowing their way ahead as the ensuing influx of humanity caused a crushing pileup at every doorway. As people began to climb over the rails seeking a way out, the increasing weight weakened the rails, causing the concrete to crack and give way. People began to fall on top of each other, collapsing into a jumbled and fatal mess.

All over downtown Chicago, the ancient buildings crumbled while the modern ones strained against the rolling force. Roads buckled and bridges rattled, swinging seemingly effortlessly like big rubber bands. The cars in the parking lot rose and fell like an ocean wave as the asphalt expanded and contracted, and then tensed and snapped, sending several cars somersaulting into the air. The droning was relentless. People in total hysteria ran about the streets not sure where to go or hide. A fast-moving crack, indulgently playful, opened and danced around the scattering people, randomly choosing who it would swallow up.

Several tourists wandered around as the shiny Bean tottered dangerously. A crying baby crawled through the forest of running feet and sat underneath the structure. One tourist noticed, ran back, and snatched up the baby before the Bean rolled off its foundation and snowballed into the crowd.

JR was engrossed in a virtual battle, his ear plugs preventing him from hearing the commotion outside, and he ignored Max's nudges and barks. He laughed triumphantly as his avatar went on a killing rampage, eliminating several of his friends. His score shot up; it was all too easy.

"You guys are wimps," he quipped.

The room rattled. JR shifted himself to get into a more comfortable position, but the place continued to sway. Confused, he looked up and his avatar on the screen instantly went up in flames. He pulled off his earplugs. The relentless swaying made him feel nauseous. He ran to the door and looked out at the panicked crowd running into each other in the hallway and then wisely decided against joining the chaos. He spun around and closed the door, trembling with realization.

"Earthquake!" JR cried.

He moved to the corner farthest away from the door and sank slowly down, burying his head and hugging his knees. Max came over and squeezed as close as possible to protect him.

"Mom…" he moaned.

Mindy burst into the room and dove for JR, pushed him against the wall, and covered him with her body just as another body-rattling quake came through. Her phone hit the ground and bounced out of sight.

⚓

Alarms rang incessantly through the ERC Center signaling a massive earthquake. The digital stopwatch on the wall started the seventy-two-hour countdown, and it was announced over the intercom; next to it, another digital display indicated the estimated magnitude of the quake.

Andre and Taylor dove into their chairs and started going through their checklists.

"Singapore's early," Taylor yelled at Andre, pulling up several data modeling and pattern-analytic charts, but Andre was not listening. He was staring at the big screen, mesmerized by the blinking red light on the world map.

"Dude," Andre said. "That can't be right."

Taylor followed his gaze. "Oh my God!" she gasped.

The blinking red light was directly on Chicago.

"Checking the coordinates again," Andre said, his voice quavering.

That's when Henry rushed in, snapping out impatiently to the pair.

"What are you still doing here? Singapore is on the other side of the world."

"Look," Taylor said, pointing to the map.

His mouth dropped when he saw the live images of Chicago landmarks popping up on several screens.

"It's not Singapore," Taylor said, unable to get the rest of the words out.

"Chicago!" Henry gasped. "But how?"

"I…maybe the New Madrid fault line bled some force off from the Yellowstone caldera," Taylor hesitantly suggested. "I just don't know…"

That's when all eyes came to focus on the second digital display on the wall; the one displaying the preliminary estimate of the magnitude of the quake. To the stunned realization of all in the room, it was displaying a number they had thought to be impossible, especially for Chicago.

10.0.

⅄

The comeback concert was in full swing. Sweat ran down Bosk's neck as he belted out a fan favorite. At first, the rattling could not be felt above the deafening music and screaming fans; then the room rolled, causing the singer to stumble. Before he could steady himself, someone screamed.

"Earthquake!"

The pyrotechnic lights ricocheted off the ceiling and walls, showering the fans. Then a grisly stampede commenced as a mad dash for the exits began, followed by the roof caving in. There was nowhere to run, no escape.

⅄

From the bleachers, Chase desperately searched the grounds for Ashlynn. He caught sight of her bright-red dress before she got swallowed up again by the crowd and then went after her, leaping over the bleachers.

"Ashlynn," Chase called out. "Wait!"

Chase grabbed the railing to steady himself but could not compete with the heaving force and lost his grip. He slammed into the wall and then slid to the floor. Fiercely he clawed up, but the floor buckled again, sending him sliding down again. He looked around for something to hold on to, anything, but the force heaved him up, slinging him over the railing. He hung suspended in the air for a moment before crashing down onto the floor of the dugout. The air exploded out of his lungs, and he was out cold.

Chapter 9

The technicians stared in morbid curiosity at the horror unfolding on the display screens.

"All right, everyone, this looks like a full ten point oh," Henry called out, once he'd shaken off his own stunned disbelief. "What do we have in Chicago?"

No one reacted.

"This is in our own backyard, and we are already behind," Henry barked.

The sudden crack of his voice, louder and more immediately threatening than any quake, snapped them out of their shock and back to business.

"Checking the resources on the ground," Andre said.

"What are the closest and best-equipped towns to take in the displaced people?" Henry asked Taylor.

Taylor pulled up a set of seismic event-density maps and quickly fed them into her analysis and predictive-analytics programs. The result would render the pattern and movement of the quake as well as how much damage this quake would do, but rendering took time. Until then, she would have to rely on her intuition to decide what areas might be safe; it had never let her down before.

"Analytics will take a few hours to render," she called back. "Until then it looks like the aftershocks are leaning toward the east. I'd say that Elgin and Aurora to the west are the best safe zones for the initial wave."

"The trauma one centers?" Henry asked.

"Milwaukee and Indianapolis," Taylor replied.

"Let's add one more," Henry said.

"Springfield just got certified, so they don't have as many experienced personnel."

"It's still good enough. Send out the alerts to the hospitals."

Then Henry turned to Andre.

"And the Robomen?"

"Chicago has…two hundred? Dude!" exclaimed Andre.

"Not a thousand?" Henry asked.

"Negative."

Taylor pointed to a memo on her screen she had brought up.

"A major recall is the culprit. Some screws used in the joints were malfunctioning. The North Carolina factories are working on replacements. Unfortunately, the workers there were on strike last week and are now playing catchup."

"On strike?" Henry asked with exasperation.

"We can pull three hundred from Seattle and five hundred from LA," Andre announced after a moment.

"ETA?"

"Seattle is five hours, and LA ten," Andre replied.

"Set those up, and get yourselves to Chicago," Henry ordered.

"Yes, sir," Andre and Taylor answered together.

The pair quickly packed up the equipment they would need and then rushed out of the room. They were almost to the door. when a technician came in with an update.

"Guys, the first analysis is in," the technician announced, "and our ten point oh has just been confirmed. It's official; we got the biggest quake on record, and it's *not* Los Angeles like we all thought it would be."

"And here I was hoping that readout was a mistake." Henry sighed.

At that moment, the main phone then rang; that same technician reached to answer it.

"It's the White House," he exclaimed. "I'm redirecting."

"Henry Newman," Henry spoke into the smartband on his upper arm a moment later.

He listened.

"Yes, definitely a ten. My best team's on it."

Henry tapped the band to hang up and then glanced up to see all eyes looking expectantly at him.

"Look," he said, "we'll have all the time to marvel at the magnitude of this later, but now, right now, we have less than seventy-two hours to secure Chicago. Where's Ben?"

"On his way home...oh my God!" gasped Taylor. "He's heading home to Chicago."

"I'll call him," Henry said. "You two *get* over to there, and set up your field station."

"Yes, sir," Taylor replied.

A swift nod, and they were both gone, soon to be on a quick flight to the Chicago area, Taylor calling ahead to arrange for everything they would need once they arrived.

⅄

An announcement came over the airplane's intercom.

"Ladies and gentlemen, we'll be starting our descent into Chicago O'Hare shortly. Please fasten your seat belts."

The flight attendant walked down the aisle checking seat belts and collecting the garbage. The plane banked sharply, and she bumped into Ben.

"Sorry, sir," she apologized.

Ben stirred; at the same time, his phone buzzed.

He opened one eye and read the incoming text message: "EMERGENCY. CALL ASAP." He connected immediately to the Control Center. "Man, Singapore's early." He yawned as he stretched.

Phones across the cabin then lit up in rapid succession, followed by the captain making an announcement over the intercom.

"Due to an emergency situation on the ground, our destination has changed. We are not landing in Chicago tonight."

Ben sat up, fully awake. "Say that again?" he spoke into the phone.

Passengers' whispers of dismay grew into anguished cries. Ben's voice trembled uncontrollably as he called up Mindy's number.

⚓

The White House conference room bustled with nervous government officials, politicians, and military personnel talking over each other. Dwight stood at the far end of the table, his hand raised to command attention.

"Stay calm, folks. This may be nothing but a few tremors the local fire departments can handle."

"We should be so lucky," Darci said as she walked in. "Guys, this is the real deal."

President Nelson entered the room behind her, wiping crumbs off his dinner jacket. "Isn't Chicago the least seismic part of the country?" he asked.

Those who were seated stood up when he entered, but he waved them back down as he quickly took his seat. He looked around, confirming the presence of his key staff members.

"You shouldn't have left your dinner, sir. I would've sent you a detailed report," Dwight said confidently.

"I'll save you the trouble. It wasn't my favorite dessert anyway."

The president turned to the Secretary of Defense Duncan Tate. Tate had his decade-old smartphone glued to his ear, waiting for the latest update on the quake. He refused to trust newer gadgets, even though he was privy to the best. He thought paranoia was a good trait to have in his profession.

"What have you got, Tate?"

"It's a ten, sir."

Everyone was silent as they weighed the implications of the disaster.

"It's been confirmed?"

"Positive," Tate replied.

There were groans of dismay.

"Oh God!" the president exclaimed, as the burden of such a magnitude of loss came down on him like a brick.

"Those scrutinizing EU hawks will swoop down on our heads in no time," Darci said.

"Since when were you scared of a little pecking?" Dwight teased.

"From the size of this, those pecks are going to be quite vicious," Darci retorted. "I'm sure several of them will try to compete for this project, just to spite us, knowing the global rules force us to comply. But our team is quite capable of handling the situation."

"You are biased, of course," Dwight said.

"Who wouldn't be?" Darci replied. "We have the best there is."

"First things first," President Nelson announced, taking charge. "God knows how many lives are in jeopardy. I must address the nation."

Chapter 10

Ben raced through the Indianapolis International Airport desperately searching for a charter-plane office. He stopped and backtracked to take another look at an advertisement that rotated up on a banner flashed up on the wall. "One Sky Jets. We get you there, early!"

A beep in his ear indicated an incoming call from Henry.

"You're already two hours behind," Henry said.

"I can make it to Chicago in one," Ben insisted. "But I can't reach Mindy. They were at the ball game."

"All communication is off, but we're trying to locate them," Henry replied.

While Ben waited for the advertisement to roll up again to get more information, he watched the social media amateur images of the destruction already streaming in on all the digital screens around him, when he noticed the young man who had sat next to him on the plane approaching him.

"The first pictures of the disaster are flooding in from survivors around the city," a reporter announced. "This is the biggest earthquake to hit American soil."

The ad finally came scrolling by again, and Ben noted the office location. He turned to start down the terminal but was stopped.

"I couldn't help overhearing you say you're going to Chicago tonight," Scott said.

"I'm in a hurry," Ben said.

"I'd like to come with you," Scott insisted.

"Look, I've got enough problems to deal with," Ben said in an irritated tone.

But Scott wasn't giving up. "I can help with the rescue effort."

Ben glanced at him, sizing him up. "And you are?"

"I created the Impala Code," Scott replied, taking off his dark glasses. "The ultimate speed for the Robomen."

Recognition suddenly flooded Ben's face as he stopped, taken aback. "You...you..."

Scott rubbed his chin. "Yep, I got rid of the beard."

Ben was surprised but quickly composed himself.

"You got rejected in the final round at the R-Three conference," he said.

"Yours truly. Scott Adams."

Scott extended his right hand, but Ben ignored it.

"You were disqualified; you stole code."

"I was framed."

"We had to start all over again and create new code because what you stole you destroyed, and then you disappeared," Ben reminded him.

"You are making this sound personal," Scott joked, but Ben had already turned away.

"The code in your Robomen has plateaued," Scott shouted after him.

Ben froze.

"You're desperate for speed," Scott continued. "China and Europe are way ahead of the United States, and you know it. You've read my thesis and publications...my code is the real deal."

Ben stood indecisively for a second and then took off running.

"What are you waiting for?" he shouted over his shoulder at Scott.

Scott quickly caught up with Ben then spoke as they both ran. "One more thing...my security clearance was suspended."

"I wouldn't have expected less," Ben replied.

Scott chuckled.

Ben and Scott rushed into the office, Ben holding up his ERC card.

"This is a national emergency. I need a plane to Chicago, now."

⅄

Dwight leaned back in his chair behind his desk in his darkened office, contemplating the surprise turn of events. The soft light from the window dimly illuminated the mementos on his desk. Prominently displayed in the center was a photo of him with a group of European delegates.

"My moment has come sooner than expected," he said to himself. "Such devastation…but every disaster has a silver lining, and now it's time to reap a great harvest…all of it under the cover of federal authority."

He reached out a hand to straighten the photo then continued his little soliloquy. He knew that lately Darci had been snooping around for more details regarding his frequent trips to Europe.

"I am the most powerful person in the country, next to the president. The only person who can threaten my position is Darci, but I think that sabotaging her ERC project will ensure that she doesn't pose a threat ever again… President Nelson has always trusted her, but I think I've finally found a way to break that trust. That will get her off my back, the profit is simply the icing on the cake."

He tapped his phone to make a call. It was time for his mole at ERC to bring up the heat.

"The plan has changed, so listen carefully," he muttered to the person listening on the other end. "Get a good-sized chunk of property this time. And while you're at it, delete all the old stuff from last week; I don't want anything from Muyang traced to me. I don't care how you do it, but put the blame on the leader."

⅄

At the field station, a hand swiped across a virtual screen on a desk. Lines of code disappeared quickly, row by row. The cursor continued blinking before a dialogue box popped up confirming the results:

"Online files erased. One copy is offline."

There was an audible and exasperated sigh.

CHAPTER 11

Chase lay in a crumpled heap in the eerie semidarkness of the Cubs dugout. He blinked and shook his head to clear the cobwebs and then struggled to sit up, but an explosion of pain hit him. He grabbed his side, groaning, and then looked down to see a splinter of railing lodged deep in his flesh, sticking out like an appendage. Chase grimaced when he saw blood on his hand.

He ripped his uniform shirt into bandage strips. Then breathing deeply, pulled out the splintered railing piece, gritting his teeth hard to suppress an anguished yelp. Chase folded one of the strips into a bandage and pressed it against the wound, securing it by wrapping the other strips around his waist before putting on his bloodied tee-shirt again. He then grabbed a Cubs jacket hanging on a hook above the player's bench and put it on to conceal the bulky bump.

He searched the bleachers again and saw Ashlynn making her way toward the family suite. He was relieved to see she remembered the drill. He raced up through the crowd to catch up with her.

"Ashlynn," he yelled.

When she turned and saw him, utter relief flooded her face. Chase ran up to her, and they embraced, Ashlynn not noticing his wince of pain.

"I'm so glad to see you," she said. "I was so scared. Are you okay?"

"Yes. You?" Chase asked.

Ashlynn nodded.

"Let's go find the others," Chase told her.

The ERC freight containers hurtled down the freeway as they moved into downtown Chicago. They crossed over the gaps and cracks in the roads effortlessly using self-replicating rails.

One container stopped outside the stadium, and the doors slid open. Robomen stepped out and marched into the stadium, the people cheering when they saw the Robomen fan out onto the field.

In the suite, a relieved Mindy hugged her children.

"Does anyone have a phone?" Mindy asked. "Mine's shattered."

Ashlynn and Chase both shook their heads.

"We lost ours," Chase told her, "and the com units in our wearables are deactivated."

They all then looked at JR; he shook his head, but no one was buying the act. He tried to slip his device into his pocket.

"Give it to me," Chase said, snatching the phone from him.

"Text Dad, then turn it off, so we can preserve power," Mindy said. "We don't know how long we're going to be here."

Ben had always insisted on at least one family member using a phone with a lithium battery backup, and Mindy was glad she listened to him and given JR her old phone and not bought him the latest gadget he had demanded.

⚔

One of the more massive freight containers stopped some distance outside of Chicago, picking a convenient field free of the presence of buildings or skyscrapers. A small squad of soldiers immediately went to work on setting things up, getting generators working, uplinking to satellites, and getting all the equipment ready that the field team would need to control the operation. By the time Taylor and Andre got off their military flight and rushed over in a personnel transport, everything was ready for them. A row of computer terminals, banks of screens and other equipment, even a small refrigerator filled with emergency snacks to keep them fed and a small attached bathroom for their other needs, as well as a small office at the end.

Taylor went to work immediately, setting up camera drones searching the crowds at Wrigley, running face recognition software, but so far getting nothing.

"No sign of the Knights," she said with obvious frustration. "What if—"

"Let's not speculate," Henry's hologram interrupted as it appeared before one of the computer terminals beside them. "If you find anything good or bad, don't mention it to Ben; at least not yet."

"God help them," Taylor said in a whispered breath.

Chapter 12

Ben checked his phone for messages as the charter plane took off. There were none from Mindy, and no call or response to his auto dial yet. He searched for any news channel on his phone that showed images of the disaster areas, hoping to pick out a familiar face at the stadium. It was unbelievable that the earthquake had happened in his town, but that his family was in the middle of it was inconceivable. He had taken every measure to secure his home for disasters. Every room had an emergency kit and an evacuation map. The basement was filled with supplies, and he had installed an earthquake shelter in the backyard.

But all that was for nothing because his family was at Wrigley Field. Their only defense was the regular drills they had reluctantly participated in at Ben's insistence whenever he was home. Though they tolerated the evacuation reminders, only JR seemed to pay much attention. He used it as an excuse to fight invisible enemies with big guns. Had the lessons been enough? He had drilled into them the importance of their designated meeting places and to never compromise that in an emergency.

On the inside, Ben was going crazy, but he had to show Henry he could do his job under this kind of stress. He had to figure out how to get himself to Wrigley as soon as he set up everything at the station. He called Henry.

"What do we have?" Ben asked as he pulled up his virtual screen.

"I'm sending you the latest right now," Henry replied.

Pictures of the damaged city filled Ben's screen. The damage to the older buildings was undeniable, but the newest reinforced buildings stood tall.

They had been built according to the code of 2035 that was set up by the United Nations for all global industrial cities of five million people and more. Chicago was one of the cities that embraced the challenge. But even with all of the care taken to come up to code, many of the older buildings had been grandfathered in due to exorbitant costs that would have bankrupted the city. Politics and powerful families with a long heritage in the area played a part in the decision. Those buildings had taken the brunt of the quake. Still, there would be people in the new buildings who would incur injuries from panic or preexisting illnesses. That number would be low, however, compared to those in the older buildings.

"The east and north areas were hit the worst," Henry said. "Mercifully, the main impact wasn't near the water, but we are still on the lookout for tsunamis."

Scott discreetly activated his Near-Field Communication sensor and pointed his phone toward Ben's screen. The same images appeared on his device.

"Whoa!" he exclaimed.

Ben zoomed in on the ravaged baseball field. "I still can't get through to Mindy," he said, trying to stay calm.

"A unit's on standby for you to use after you set up the operation," Henry said, trying to reassure him.

Henry knew his friend was under great stress, but national security came first; it depended on Ben executing his job flawlessly for the next few hours or so, and Henry was ready to take extreme steps to ensure the job got done.

Suddenly Ben's phone buzzed. It was a text from JR's phone.

He felt dizzy with relief; then he leaned back and closed his eyes. His anxiety abated, but his stomach kept churning. He was more desperate than ever to get to them, but now he could concentrate on the task at hand. Ben was naturally competitive and ready for the challenge; there was no room for error. His plan was to get into the field as soon as he landed and dictate action to the station from there. Taylor and Andre would take instructions remotely from him. They had done this many times before.

The images on Ben's screen were replaced by a breaking-news banner, then the grim face of President Nelson.

"As you have already heard and seen, an earthquake has hit Chicago. Every effort is being made to rescue people and save lives," the president said and paused for effect. "For two years after the big LA earthquake, we have been testing the ERC disaster recovery program. It has not been put to the test on American soil, until now. Miss Woods?"

Darci stepped up to the podium.

"There are going to be three phases of this operation: Search and Rescue, Aid, and Reconstruction. The first seventy-two hours are crucial for this operation to succeed within which the Robomen will complete all search-and-rescue activities. Once they have accomplished their tasks, organizations will be allowed to bring in aid and assistance into the Chicago area. After that, reconstruction will commence. We want to get Chicago back on its feet as soon as possible."

Ben snapped his phone shut and then anxiously waited out the rest of the flight. A short time later, he and Scott stepped off the plane and were immediately surrounded by soldiers.

"What's this all about?" Ben angrily asked.

"Come with us, sir! We're to escort you to the field station."

"Wow! I didn't know you were such a big shot," Scott said.

Ben was fit to be tied. He knew Henry wanted to make sure he did not divert from a task of such huge national interest. In moments, he and Scott were shuttled into a waiting military helicopter.

CHAPTER 13

Taylor was so relieved to see Ben walk into the station that she didn't notice Scott at first.

"Your signature is required for the tremor-modeling specs," she began, handing him an electronic pad. "They are moving as expected, and I'm rendering all the information now to get the ETA on the aftershocks."

Ben scribbled his signature on the pad and handed it back to Taylor.

"We have to be careful what we tell the media at this point. Release only the necessary information," Ben told her.

"Any communication from your family?" she asked. "There's signal interference in space causing interruption in the wearable technology, but I'm scanning every face in the field using an older software version, and Andre's tracking the phones."

"Thanks," Ben replied, managing a weak smile. "They're in the family suite. They've done enough drills to know that in such a situation they stay put until help arrives."

"I know you want to be with them, and Henry shouldn't have brought you in here like this," Taylor told him. "He must be off his rocker!"

"I understand why he did it," Ben told her, "but I'm leaving as soon as I have set things up."

Ben glanced at the clock and then continued, "You and I know he did the right thing. Have you confirmed the time of the first big aftershock?"

"Not yet. From what I can glean off my analysis, it's no sooner than seventy-two hours," Taylor said.

Ben nodded. He tended to agree with Taylor in these matters as there were few people in her field who knew more about analyzing earthquake patterns.

Scott had wandered off and was studying one of the screens on the wall that projected Taylor's calculations and data. "The setup for your predictive analysis is too slow," he said. "I can make it go faster."

"Excuse me?" Taylor bristled. For the first time, she looked at Scott directly. He looked vaguely familiar, but for the life of her she could not recall where she had seen him, and this wasn't the moment to find out. He had just insulted her. Andre, likewise, took an instant dislike to him and eyed him with suspicion.

"Everyone," Ben said. "This is Scott Adams. He'll be working with us."

Scott had already figured out which station was Taylor's. He sat down in her chair, took control of her computer, and began typing away. Taylor could not believe the intrusion and turned to Ben in disgust.

"Ben, we don't have time for this nonsense."

"He knows what he's doing. Plus, I have a plan," Ben explained as he walked toward the small office at the end of the container, Taylor following in his wake.

"Well, what's the plan?" Taylor pressed.

"Give him full clearance," Ben said.

"What? Full clearance?"

"You heard me."

"Come and see," Scott then called out to them. "It's your birthday! I just saved you three hours of twiddling your thumbs. I eliminated the reverberations and echoes and that sped up the rendering. By the way, the aftershock strikes in...forty-eight hours."

Taylor was intrigued. She returned to her station to take a look at his work. Who was this guy? Taylor reluctantly peered over his shoulder, mentally running through his calculations. Not only was it in forty-eight hours, but also its epicenter was right in the middle of Chicago.

"It can't be," Taylor said.

"What can't be? My speed or the aftershock?" Scott said.

Unable to shake the annoyance, it took all she had not to slap his face. But he was right on both accounts.

"Whatever." She shrugged.

Scott chuckled.

Henry's hologram had been observing the new teammate, and he was livid. He knew exactly who Scott was and had never trusted the guy. Scott was a loose cannon and spelled trouble wherever he went. Ben, though, seemed serenely oblivious to it.

Henry tapped his shoulder, dialing in Ben.

"A word with you," he said.

In the office, Ben faced Henry's hologram.

"You have no right to make an executive decision without consulting me first," Henry said with very evident displeasure in his voice.

"That makes us even, Henry," Ben continued. "You didn't have to go to the extreme herding us in with the soldiers. My word is good enough."

"My mistake," Henry briskly replied. "So what's his story?"

"He offered his help while I was getting the charter, and there was no time to call you. Plus, we need him desperately if we're to pull this off."

"You're jeopardizing this operation by bringing in someone we have never worked with. Worse, he's a thief, and you know it."

"We aren't going to make it without more speed, and we already have several problems to deal with, including the first big aftershock striking sooner than expected."

"With the additional Robomen on the way, we will manage well enough."

"If we stay at our normal pace," Ben snapped back, "even in the best scenario, there's going to be more loss of life than you and I can live with. His code will speed up the Robomen."

"But you can't—you know that—okay, so you're right," Henry finally admitted. "But my eye's on him. I bet we'll find out the real reason he's here sooner or later."

Back in the main room, Taylor showed Andre an article on her screen.

"Remember R-Three two years ago?" she whispered. "That's him. He was accused of stealing the Impala Code from the Polish scientist, Leon Weigl. It's the fastest machine code on the planet."

Andre's face turned white as realization hit him; then fear washed over him.

"He's a code mercenary, among other things," Taylor continued. "And I just gave him clearance. What's Ben thinking?"

If Scott was aware of the hostility toward him, he did not show it. He was now situated in his own workspace and already testing his code. He was in his elements and enjoying every minute of Taylor's discomfort. She was smart and competitive, and he liked that. He also liked that he finally had the perfect opportunity to implement the code he had hidden from the world for so long. The timing was almost too perfect. He nodded to the technician assigned to him.

"Try it now."

The technician switched on his Brain Interface Cap and then moved his head from left to right. The virtual Roboman's movements blurred in a vision of speed. The technician was impressed.

"Whoa! How did you do that?"

Ben came over to watch the progress and observed the transformation. He knew that he had made the right decision bringing in Scott.

"How fast?"

"Ten times faster while using the same amount of energy," Scott said. "After the training period and the machine's learning multiplies, the speed will be even greater."

"It shaves off minutes, if not hours. This is absolutely amazing," Ben exclaimed, very much impressed as he slapped Scott on the back. "Good work!"

"I've been waiting a long time to show this off." Scott shrugged.

"Do a few more virtual tests," Ben told him. "If they're clean, I'll get Henry to take a look and get clearance to test it out in the field."

A

Survivors stepped off the trolleys and were welcomed by Robomen, who guided them to their new lodgings in the safe zone. The honeycomb structures were up and ready to receive them. A Roboman scanned their fingerprints for identification; then each was handed an emergency package by an assistant robot before stepping into their temporary homes. Several news broadcast teams had already set up camp vying for the best vantage spot in front of the bamboo-tent city.

Bly Cochrane, the retro blond journalist, was up front and center.

"This is the first temporary refuge," she said. "The first residents have affectionately named it the Hive City. We have been reassured it's in an area where the least aftershocks are expected."

◢

In the Oval Office, President Nelson and Darci watched the drama unfold from several screens showing the different news output of the rescue efforts in Chicago. Aides fielded the constant stream of interruptions from the calls from world leaders offering their help and support.

"Can they pull this off in the set time?" the president anxiously asked.

"It's still too early to tell, sir," Darci replied.

"It won't take long for the people to complain we're too slow."

"You are going to do what you do best," Darci told him. "Keeping the public's attention on you with your humanitarian activities will build trust. The plan is to keep you out of any operations of which you should not be aware."

President Nelson smiled; he got the point. His job was to focus on keeping the nation assured and confident while the search and rescue operations did whatever must be done behind the scenes to move things forward. Of course, the usual plausible deniability was a very necessary thing in this day and age. But once in a while, he wished he could know exactly what was going on instead of being briefed after the fact, if at all. Yet, he trusted the men and women who were strategically placed around him. He knew they were the ones who controlled this show, and he was only a puppet spokesman. If he was honest with himself, it was a good arrangement, and with such disasters he would have it no other way.

"Hugging babies is one of my favorite duties as a president," he said as he shrugged. "It never grows old."

A

Ben panned across Wrigley Field, looking for the best group of Robomen to test. Though the rest of his team was skeptical about trying this on the field, they trusted Ben and knew he would not do anything to jeopardize the operation.

"Let's try the code on this group of five Robomen working on the east side of the field," Ben decided.

Andre selected the group on his computer and hit the Execute key. A progress bar raced across the screen to show the code had downloaded into the Robomen. As the guys watched, the Robomen started moving faster. At first, it was a minor change, then they quickly gained more speed, and yet their precision did not erode. The Robomen's movements blurred as they increased in effectiveness. Everyone watched a Roboman move a boulder out of the way to get to a trapped person in seconds. In spite of himself, Andre was impressed.

"Let's do one more test," Ben said. "How about the group in the bleachers on the south side? If it shows the same results, we'll expand to the rest of the field."

Ben couldn't have been more pleased with the outcome. Funny how rules flew out the window when disaster strikes. Normal protocol would have prevented Scott from setting a foot in this station, but the same people now turned a blind eye to his past and notoriety. Henry was skeptical at first but would come around quickly given the great results. He was doing everything he could to ensure the White House did not block what they were working on.

Things were finally settling into a manageable routine. The Robomen worked with amazing speed around the field in the night. There had been no emergencies in the past hour, and they were on schedule, which meant the team could relax a little. Scott took a bathroom break while Ben set about assuring Henry his team had everything in control. It was time to get out to the field and find his family.

Looking around to make sure no one was watching him, Andre pulled out his phone; then he searched for a hidden file and dragged it off his phone and dropped it onto his virtual screen. He looked around again to make sure his actions had gone unnoticed and then hit the Execute button, and the program started loading.

Across the room, Ben was now talking to Taylor.

"I'm heading out," he told her. "I'll command from the field. I need you to lead here."

"Sure. It's the usual drill, isn't it?" Taylor laughed nervously. She wanted nothing more than to reassure Ben that he could leave.

"Exactly," Ben said.

"Then you have nothing to worry about," Taylor told him.

"I should be back before countdown."

"Be safe," Taylor called after him.

But Ben had not made it to the door when an alarm went off.

"It's Wrigley," Taylor said as she zoomed in on the field on her screen. "Something's up on the east side."

A Roboman yanked out a row of seats, swung it in a mighty arc, and sent it flying toward a group of people. The coach of the visiting team ran in front of the Robomen, waved his arms, shouting at him to stop, but the Roboman took hold of the man and hurled him into the air.

People screamed in fear and scattered trying to get away from the advancing Roboman. The trapped group ran to the end of the field, but there was no escape except to go up the low concrete wall, which they desperately began to do. It was easy to climb, but the panic caused such a stampede that those who didn't make it over or lost their grip got crushed under the feet of others.

Ben watched in horror at what was happening on the screens as Taylor looked accusingly at Scott. "The Robomen are compromised. Obviously, it's the code you installed."

"That's not possible!" Scott exclaimed.

"Did you test for regression?" Ben asked.

"Of course, I did. Several times."

Ben was not sure if he was telling the truth and finally just shook his head.

"We have no choice but to uninstall."

"It's not the code," Scott insisted.

Henry's hologram materialized; he had heard enough.

"We don't need your services anymore," he said coldly to Scott. "The guards will escort you out."

"I have jurisdiction over this field station," Ben protested. "He's not going anywhere. At least not until we figure out the problem. We can reset and run it again.

"That takes time, which you don't have," Henry said. "Andre will take it from here and reset to our original code."

Andre grinned with obvious pleasure.

Ben looked at the clock in anguish. He knew that whatever time they had gained would be eaten up shortly. Cleaning up this mess would set them back even more. The most important thing, however, was to make sure the corrupted code did not get into the cloud, replicate, and infect other Robomen. That would cause a deadly downward spiral and totally knock the operation off its feet.

Scott walked up to Andre's screen to take a closer look. Andre glanced at him suspiciously, instantly defensive. Was Scott trying to intimidate him? After all, wasn't this mess his fault? But Scott had only paused for a second and then walked on. He walked back to his desk, closed his computer, folded his arms, and closed his eyes. His mind was already elsewhere.

"We'll get Delta Force to shield the people while I do a manual reset," Ben said, trying to salvage the situation with Henry.

"How many Robomen do you think you'll get to before they catch on?" Henry said.

"We can't start destroying them now," Ben said.

"You should've thought of that before you went maverick. We cut our losses now and clean up this mess," Henry commanded.

Clearly, there was no changing Henry's mind. Ben had to think of another strategy. He needed to find out what the real issue was, if it wasn't the code, and before Scott left. What else was he missing? Ben walked over to Taylor.

"Check the last data log," Ben whispered.

Taylor obliged.

"Data one, show data log one," Taylor said.

A chart popped up. All was green.

"Check the backup."

"Data one, show data log two."

There was no chart.

"Odd. Data one, show data log two," Taylor said.

Taylor pulled up a virtual keyboard and typed a command.

"It's gone!"

"Search all the servers," Ben said.

Taylor typed some more. "Nothing."

"Who was the last person to access it?"

She scanned the name log.

"It was you. You did an offline sync yesterday for the Muyang data," Taylor replied, clearly frightened. "Ben, what's going on?"

Ben felt the blood rush from his face.

"Don't say anything. Not yet."

Ben was desperate now. He was wasting precious time and not anywhere nearer to his family. He walked over to Henry's hologram.

"Look, I can take care of this a whole lot better if I'm in the field. That's what I've always done. Why should it be any different this time? Is it because it's on American soil?"

"You are staying put. It's a command," Henry said. "This is a national emergency."

"I won't abandon my family," Ben said.

"Hey guys," Andre said, cutting in. "The number of clean Robomen waiting to be assigned has dwindled to less than twenty. Reinforcements are still a couple of hours away. Where do I deploy the last ones?"

"The Obama Museum in Jackson Park has eight hundred people, including several international delegates who are stranded," Taylor responded, "but the ground is stable there, and the police are managing the crowd. The Atrium Mall is the most populated place after the field. There are almost two thousand people trapped. It was opening night for a shoe sale for a hot new designer. On top of that, there was an oldie concert, and it was a sold-out show...Brandon Bosk? I think that's it. Several levels of the mall have collapsed, trapping hundreds."

"You know the protocol, Ben. Make the call," Henry said.

"Taylor's got this," Ben said.

"Don't force me to do this," Henry said tersely.

"Let him go, Henry," Taylor said.

Ben walked away.

Henry was unwavering and tapped his smartband. "You leave me no choice," he called after Ben.

Two armed officers entered and stood guard at the doors.

"This is silly," Ben said with a shake of his head. "You can't keep me here."

"Don't tempt me," Henry said.

"Ben, please," Taylor pleaded, "just call it. We need all the time we can get."

"Send them to the mall," Ben said as he glared down at Henry's image.

Immediately everyone sprang into action.

"All right guys," Andre announced, "sending the remaining units to the mall."

Ben stared at the central screen, desperately scanning the faces on the field, before walking into the bathroom.

Meanwhile, in the family suite, Chase looked up at the ceiling. The paint was cracking, and dust particles were falling from the ceiling all around the family. The commotion on the field was growing louder as JR covered his ears and hid his face in Mindy's lap. Without his medication, there was no telling how he would react to the unrelenting stimuli. They had to find a quiet place.

"We can't stay here." Chase decided.

Ben stared at his gaunt face in the bathroom mirror and then sank to the floor unable to control his stomach's dry heaves. He had spent years trying to suppress the past, but in this moment, the pain came crushing down on him. In the years with Mindy, he thought he had dealt with the secrets of his past, but he knew he could never forgive himself. As far as Mindy knew, the loss of both his first wife and child was a memory too painful for him to talk about, and so she left it at that. What she didn't know was that he had abandoned his son when he needed him the most. He had promised himself this would never happen again.

"Please God...I'm so sorry...Mindy..." Ben cried.

Ben fought the waves of despair that threatened to overwhelm him, pulled himself up, and breathed in deeply. He willed himself to calm down as he exhaled.

A knock on the door startled him. He wiped away the tears, ran his fingers through his hair, and opened the door. Scott swooped past him.

"It's not the code," Scott said.

"You've said that before," Ben snorted.

"The issue's in the plumbing. It's deep in the private cloud," Scott continued.

"Our cloud's impenetrable," Ben said. "Our sandboxing is state of the art the air gaps are solid."

"Oh, it's foolproof, all right, which means one thing," Scott said.

"Impossible." Ben gasped.

The implication was too obvious.

"You have a mole." Scott nodded.

"I handpicked this team and didn't make it easy on them," Ben insisted.

"Unfortunately, one of them, someone with full administrative access, created a chameleon with an exceptional cloak. I almost missed it because it customizes rapidly in any situation, and it cleans up after itself pretty well. Quite impressive."

Ben groaned in frustration. He sensed that Scott was right. Still, it was hard to comprehend that someone on the team had compromised the system.

"Can you destroy it?"

"I need time to find out its patterns, habits, what it delivers, how and when it exits," Scott replied. "Also, there's a risk that it leaves traps behind. If so, I need to circumvent them."

"It's time we don't have," Ben said as he paced the room. "But why? Why now?"

"The usual. Money, power, or both. But finding the mole will have to wait. Getting the Robomen working is my first priority."

"Why try to destroy this operation?" Ben mumbled.

"Someone might be after the company, or even the government. It's the perfect opportunity for sabotage," Scott said.

Ben was quiet for a while, but his pacing continued.

"Wondering if you can trust me?" Scott asked.

Ben stopped and glared at Scott. "Should I?"

"I'm not the mole," Scott answered. "Obviously, you aren't either. You're way too miserable."

Ben wiped his tired face. "Someone's trying to frame me."

"You mean the missing data log," Scott said.

Ben nodded, at the same time wondering how he found that out.

"Your code's solid?" Ben asked.

"You've already seen what it can do," Scott said.

"Then we'll use it, but not yet," Ben said. "At any time, the rogue code could spread to all the Robomen in the field then the city. Can't imagine what would happen if we added speed to this mess."

"I'll get to work,"

"Be discreet."

"I wouldn't have it any other way."

CHAPTER 14

Chase opened the door of the suite and looked out into the empty hallway. The lights were flickering, making the place look sinister, but it was safe to venture out. The floor looked stable with no visible cracks. He beckoned the family to follow him.

They hadn't gone far when Ashlynn, who was in the rear, heard a whisper coming from below her. Curious, she looked down over the rail into the stands below. To her surprise there was a woman dangling, swinging slowly in midair, barely holding on to the edge of the floor with her fingertips.

"Please, help me," the woman whispered desperately.

"Ashlynn, come on!" Chase called out to her. The family had reached the stairway and was about to go down.

Torn, Ashlynn couldn't tear her eyes away from the woman, but she knew she wasn't strong enough to save the women, so she shook her head and started walking away.

"I'm sorry," said Ashlynn.

"I can't hold on much longer…please," the woman pleaded, calling after her.

Ashlynn stopped and shouted to her family.

"There's a woman over here. We've got to help her," Ashlynn shouted, walking back. "She's going to fall any second."

"Ashlynn, come here," Mindy commanded, but Ashlynn ignored her. Knowing how impulsive she was, Chase raced toward his sister.

"Ashlynn, wait," Chase shouted.

Ashlynn steadied herself against the railing, leaned over, and offered her hand to the woman. The woman mustered all her remaining strength, let go of one hand, and grabbed Ashlynn's hand. Ashlynn pulled up with all her might and the woman was able to get a hold of the railing with her other hand, but it was already weakened and unable to hold the weight of both women; it started folding. Ashlynn knew she could not hold on much longer. Desperately, the woman tried to lift up one leg to grip the edge, but she hit empty air causing her grip to slip dangerously.

"Please, don't let me fall," the woman screamed.

Ashlynn started sliding toward the edge and knew she had to pull back, but the woman had a death grip on her. She cried out, Chase reaching to grab hold of her legs, but the railing snapped, and Ashlynn went over the edge. The women fell past the stands, disappearing into the belly of the stadium.

With the terrified screams ringing in his ears, Chase raced back to the stairs, taking two steps at a time. Max flew past him while JR and Mindy followed as fast as they could.

Chase tried to adjust to the semidarkness of the basement. There was dust and debris all over but no sign of the women. Max, however, had already located them and started digging.

Then Chase heard a faint moan.

"Ashlynn?"

Chase attacked the rubble with Max, using his bare hands in a total panic, ignoring the pain from the cuts. Chase made a small opening that allowed a glimpse of Ashlynn's face still barely visible. Eight-foot bamboo beams had saved Ashlynn from being crushed by the weight of the debris. The poor woman was not as fortunate.

"You all right?" Chase asked.

"My leg. I can't move it. It hurts," Ashlynn groaned.

"We'll get you out in no time."

Chase and Mindy exchanged a worried look. The beams that saved her life had also trapped her in a wooden cocoon. Chase pushed against the beam, but it didn't yield.

"I'll go look for an ax," Chase said.

"Don't leave me," Ashlynn cried.

"No one's going anywhere," Mindy said.

⋏

Chase's footsteps echoed through the dimly lit basement tunnel. Using the light of the emergency exit signs, watching for cracks in the floor and fallen objects blocking his path, he felt his way along the wall until he found a door. He opened it, and the light flickered on. It was a closet with brooms, buckets, other janitorial and moving stuff, but no ax.

Leaving the closet door open to feed more light into the hallway, he walked farther down and turned a corner. In the distance, right below an exit sign, he saw an ax secured in a wall cabinet above a first-aid box and fire extinguisher. But there was a large three-foot crack in the ground spanning the width of the hallway and separating him from his desired object. No way for him to tell how deep it was or if there was any exposed electrical cabling, he would just have to jump it.

Back at the closet, Chase pushed away several boxes that were mounted on a rolling dolly. He stood on top of it, testing it with his weight. It would do as a makeshift old-fashioned skateboard. It was the next best thing to a hoverboard.

In the hallway, Chase positioned himself a few feet away from the crack, took a deep breath and pushed off. Building speed, he launched into the air, flew over the crack, and landed hard on the other side, doubling over in pain. In the excitement, he had forgotten about his injury.

Chase clutched his throbbing side while he rummaged through the first-aid box. He found a bottle of painkillers and popped a couple of pills into his mouth. Then he unwrapped the strips; the wound had bled through the bandage. He made a new generous bandage from the gauze he found in the box and rewrapped his side and then stuffed the rest of the gauze in a bag and slung it over his back.

He saw something move in the corner of his eye and so turned, his heart pounding. A dog jumped him, knocking him over. He coiled his body, ready to kick out, but instead the dog licked him all over. It was Max!

"Max! You followed me…no, Mom must have sent you."

Max barked.

"You should have stayed with the others, but glad to see you."

Chase tied the ax to his back by using the extra straps he pulled from his backpack. He tugged them to confirm the ax was secure and then jumped on his makeshift skateboard. His right leg pumping, he pushed the board to full speed and then skidded to a stop, inches from the edge.

Max flew past him, landing easily on the other side.

Chase moved back as far as he could, took a deep breath, whipping the skateboard to an even faster speed, and launched into the air over the crack. The dolly nipped the edge and then careened off in the darkness. Chase grabbed the edge with one hand, swung up, and hooked the edge with his heel. The ax, however, began to slip down his back; the strap was loosening.

"Max, the ax. Get the ax," Chase shouted.

Max scrambled toward him, carefully approaching the edge.

The dog snatched hold of the ax handle and pulled it to safety. Chase pulled himself onto the floor and rolled onto his back, exhausted, the throbbing pain in his side shouting for attention.

CHAPTER 15

Wolf's empty stomach growled, but he knew he couldn't keep anything down if he tried to eat. The screams of dying people haunted him, yet he could not turn away from looking at the pandemonium at Wrigley Field. In a few minutes, he would have to make a decision that would bring the angst of the American people solidly on him. Tate and his team had already briefed him on the consequences of taking no action versus a list of options to get the situation under control, and were now on their way to the conference room for the final decision. But first, Wolf needed to speak with Tate privately. He had asked him to stop by the Oval Office, so he could gauge the reaction on his face without a group of officers breathing down his neck.

Tate was ushered into the room quickly followed by Dwight. The president frowned, but Dwight was oblivious to the fact that he was uninvited.

"This can't go on," Dwight began. "The corrupt code will get to the cloud any second, and we can't risk all the robots becoming compromised."

The president turned to Tate to get his opinion. "What do you think?"

"We have to go in full force and take out the rogues quickly." Tate agreed.

"And the loss of life?"

"It will be worse if you don't go in now and aggressively," Dwight advised. "It's only a matter of time before the rest of the fleet gets infected with the corrupted code, and they will take over the city."

"After looking at all the viable options," Tate nodded and said, "there is only one that will get the results we are looking for."

"All right"—the president sighed heavily—"if there is no other way, then it must be done."

⋏

Ben was focused on coming up with a plan to remove the dysfunctional Robomen. While he wanted to get the project back on the clock, he also wanted to give Scott as much time as he needed to find the mole. He worked out scenario after scenario, until he finally felt he had something solid to present to Henry. The loss of the Robomen seemed inevitable, but that could be minimized.

He was just about to call Henry, when this phone rang.

"Hey, you beat me to it." Ben smiled at how they were able to read each other's mind.

"I'm sorry, Ben. Just got a call from the top. We're done."

"What?"

"The military's taking over the field. They're going to take out the rogues before they multiply all over Chicago," Henry said, resigned.

"How are they going to do it?" Ben said. "By using hand-to-hand combat? Nah! Air to land missile—"

"Don't," Henry said.

"Do you care at all…about us winning out there? They're going to destroy all of them indiscriminately. My family's still in there."

"The decision has been made," Henry said. "I am not in control anymore."

⋏

Mindy dug around Ashlynn's leg, steadily breaking through the rubble while Chase worked on splitting the beam over them with the ax. Chase kept an eye on JR, who despite his running nose, hugged Max tightly. He would not let the dog out of his sight but was bored. He looked around to see no one was paying attention to him and then dragged his mother's jacket slowly toward him. He pulled out his phone from the pocket and turned it on, but Chase was onto him already.

"Turn it off right now. It's not time to contact Dad," Chase said.

"I'm bored," JR said.

"Look, I'll let you send the SOS, but it's not time yet," Mindy said.

Mindy knew she had to come up with something quickly to keep JR busy; something that would hold his attention for a good length of time.

"Hey, JR," Chase said, pausing at his digging, "why don't you and Max build us a fortress to protect us from the bad guys? You can use my skateboard for the tower."

JR's eyes lit up, and Mindy shot Chase a look of gratitude.

⟁

Andre was slightly unnerved when he saw Ben come out of his office and walk toward him. He swiped to another page to cover up what he was really working on and then waited for Ben to walk past him before switching back to his initial page. He was looking for the offline file that was the last piece of evidence connecting him to any robotic malfunction. He had set up a search program checking every few minutes to see if his spider had found something and then almost fell off his chair when he saw the blinking location and its coordinates.

It was at Wrigley Field; someone at the game had downloaded the file. But how could that be? Who would—Ben? It had to be Ben. He must have unwittingly downloaded a copy to one of his family's devices.

"Bingo!" Andre whispered.

Chapter 16

D arci entered Dwight's office unannounced. She was furious she had been left out of the loop about the secret meeting and suspected it was Dwight who crossed her name off that list. Granted, she'd been at the United Nations building, answering questions about the quake. By the time she had returned, the meeting was adjourned. Her top aide caught wind of it and briefed her about the decision. Dwight, preparing to leave his office with his entourage, was not pleased when he saw her.

"You'd be wise to get out of my way," Dwight growled.

"Why don't you let those guys do their job?" Darci said.

"Wake up, Darci. They messed up!"

The aides nudged Darci out of the way while Dwight continued to walk down the hallway, Darci following.

"The president can still call off the Special Forces," Darci said.

"You are too late," Dwight said.

"You're sending them out there to die. Robomen are engineered to protect themselves."

"A price must be paid, Miss Woods."

"You can't hide it from the world."

"Oh, we're taking care of that."

Darci was horrified. Dwight had gone too far.

"You're tampering with the media too? Looping the last piece of good news over and over again, aren't you? How many minutes will it take before they realize they aren't seeing live footage? How many rules are you going to break before you realize the consequences?" Darci shouted after him.

"I am not feeding the people any miscommunication, just delaying the newsfeed a few minutes and editing it appropriately," Dwight stopped, looking straight at Darci. "You said it yourself, Miss Woods. Hope is an invaluable thing."

Dwight had clearly won this round; he could barely suppress a satisfied smirk. So far things were going smoothly, just as he'd planned. He would keep shaking the tree and sooner or later whatever she was hiding, or whatever she was protecting, all would be revealed.

▲

At the field station, Ben and his team watched the screens with increasing dread as the Special Forces secured several areas at the stadium. Ben did not know whether to scream or cry. He was getting frantic about his family's whereabouts. He texted them to get out of the suite and away from the field as far as possible, but he had not been able to track them since they let him know they were safe in the suite. He watched as the squad of soldiers bravely engaged the Robomen but were no match for the big machines, whose instincts were flawless when they detected danger. The men were quickly overpowered and destroyed.

"Stupid, stupid," Ben muttered.

The snipers were not safe either at the top of the stadium's roof. They had landed silently and were moving quickly into position, but they didn't see the Roboman coming up behind them.

A Roboman grabbed one sniper and snapped his neck like a twig. The other snipers dropped their weapons and fled.

He had to get out there as fast as possible. The easy part was outsmarting the guards stationed at the door. Waiting for Scott to give the green light was the nightmare. He had no control on what he was doing.

Andre watched these new events with excitement. This was the moment. He made his decision and quickly typed the preset commands he had prepared, ahead of time, using the virtual keyboard on his palm.

"Sending two, so they can figure things out faster," he muttered to himself. "Thank God for dual neural networks."

He took full control of two rogue Robomen; they turned and left the field. They jumped over the wall, dropped down onto Clark Street, and walked along the outside wall of the field, heading toward Andre's preestablished coordinates.

⋏

Ben and Henry's hologram literally faced off at each other's throats.

"I won't allow this to continue," Ben threatened.

"Don't you get it? We lost control the minute the Robomen went rogue," Henry said.

"We can turn this around."

"Ben, you are no longer in control," Henry told him. "Wake up!"

"You're right," Ben said. "You can wait. But I won't be a spectator to a double disaster."

From the corner of his eye, Ben caught Taylor anxiously beckoning him over to her desk.

"Hey, guys. Something's up."

The remaining soldiers were on the run. "Go! Go! Go!" The commander of the group screamed covering their retreat out of the stadium with blasts of rapid heavy artillery fire.

"Whoa! That's a fast retreat if I ever saw one," Taylor said.

Ben knew from his past military experience that these abrupt changes were always a sign that something big was about to happen. He felt a familiar tingling in the back of his neck and then heard a shrill sound that echoed through the station before a blinding light covered the field area. Ben's eyes widened as he watched a stealth aircraft fly over the field. It had released a flare that careened down the field.

"A rocket," he whispered in disbelief.

Then...BOOM!

⋏

The rocket exploded in the middle of the field. The explosion was so loud that Taylor instinctively flinched. Fireball upon fireball smashed across the field. Robomen melted, and humans vaporized.

In the stadium basement, Chase, JR, and Mindy were knocked off their feet.

⋏

An eerie silence engulfed the office.

Ben's hologram burst into Henry's office barely controlling his rage.

"When were you planning to tell me?" screamed Ben.

"I didn't think they would go to that extent," Henry answered.

"Nonsense," Ben shouted. "We trust each other."

"Do we?" Henry said.

"Do we what? Do you doubt my trust in you? Is this about Scott and his code?"

"You know the bad code is starting to replicate, and that has to be stopped, otherwise the entire city of Chicago is going to be taken over by the rogue Robomen," Henry stated. "Why didn't you tell me about yesterday's data sync?"

"The data," Ben said, surprised. "What are you implying?"

"Can you explain why it's missing?"

Ben shook his head in disbelief. Henry was accusing him of sabotage in his own company. He pulled off his badge and placed it on the table.

"What are you doing? We've got to finish this," Henry said.

"Oh no, I don't," Ben replied.

"Don't do this. You can't walk away. Ben!"

Ben's hologram faded away. Instinctively, Henry grabbed after him, catching empty air. Panic flooded Henry's face; veins bulged in his temples. He barked into his phone, "Get me a flight to Chicago. Now!"

Scott nodded to Ben as he walked by. That is what Ben has been waiting for.

"Bathroom in five. I need to make a call first." Ben whispered to Scott.

"What's going on, Ben?" asked Taylor.

Ben shook his head.

"Not now."

Scott cleared his desk, gathered what he thought he would need for the trip, and headed for the bathroom, but Taylor blocked him.

"Where are you going?" Taylor demanded.

"Out to dinner. I hear the sushi in this area is to die for."

Unable to get anything from Ben, Taylor then thought she would get some answers from Scott. "Why did you hack into the subsystems using the logistics computer?"

"I did?" Scott replied.

"I'm not stupid," Taylor told him.

"You know, he's not going to leave his wife."

Taylor flared up at the rude jab. "What did you say?"

"Ben loves his wife," Scott said.

Taylor slapped him. "How dare you?"

Scott rubbed his cheek, smiled slowly, and walked away without another word, leaving Taylor fuming. She knew it was no use trying to get him to apologize. As much as she hated admitting it, he was right. She admired Ben; no, she loved him. Conflicting emotions washed over Taylor's face.

Andre walked up, looking after Scott. "What was that about?"

"None of your business," Taylor said.

⚔

Darci was in the car, on her way to yet another meeting, where she would be explaining the repercussions of the government's decision, when Ben's call came in. She frowned as she answered it.

"How did you get this number?" Darci said.

Ben ignored her. "The truth, Darci. I want the truth."

"What are you talking about?"

"There's going to be a second round, isn't there?" Ben said. "You're going to destroy the whole stadium. No one wants the rogue machines to transmit the corrupted code to the rest of the Robomen, but there has to be another way."

"I don't know anything," Darci replied. "I wasn't invited to the luau."

"Both of us know you're lying. Please don't let it happen. I can turn this around. You don't want to deal with the financial fallout, let alone the unnecessary loss of human life this decision will cause."

"I'm not sure what can be done at this point," Darci said.

"Talk to Nelson."

"And tell him what?"

"Not to do what I think he's going to do...I'm begging you...my family's in there!"

"All right." She sighed. "I'll try."

"One hour," Ben said.

"I can't promise anything," Darci protested.

"One hour, Darci," Ben repeated.

CHAPTER 17

Scott rolled a new set of prints onto his fingertips, waited for the adhesive to dry, and tested them under a stream of water. Ben walked into the bathroom as he was finishing up.

"The code is ready when you are," Scott said as he calmly dried his hands.

"I'm going in to get my family."

"I'm coming with you," Scott said.

"I need you here to install the code," Ben insisted.

"I can access it anywhere." Scott assured him. "By the way, did I mention I picked up your family's signal a few minutes ago?"

Ben was equally surprised and relieved. "Why didn't you tell me as soon as you traced them? They are safe? Where are they?"

"They're below ground but still in the stadium. One other person picked up the signal too, and I was hoping it was you."

Ben shook his head.

"Then believe me; you'll need me with you."

"It is most likely the mole," Ben said. "Not sure what he or she wants. You won't tell a soul; not Henry, not Andre, not—"

"Taylor's clean," Scott said.

"How do you know?"

"I have my ways."

"How close are you to finding the person?"

"Soon enough, I hope," Scott admitted. "My sinkhole has caught diddly-squat."

"Maybe you need to set an ambush," Ben suggested.

"Right. But we have a bigger problem with the Robomen. Say I hijack a Roboman's circuit, replace its code, and beam it into the mothership, and voila, self-replicating to all in seconds."

Ben couldn't resist a smile. Scott made it sound so easy.

"All right, first things first. Let's get you out of here and get you a Roboman," Ben said. "We have to be careful. The military is on red alert now and will stop anyone coming into the area."

▲

Chase scrambled up from where he had fallen from the force of the blast.

"What just happened?" Ashlynn asked between sobs.

"That wasn't an aftershock," Chase said, brushing off the dust.

"You gotta get me out of here. Please get me out," Ashlynn said, her voice rising to near hysteria.

Mindy crawled into a gap in the rubble to reach out her hand to her. "It's going to be all right, baby."

▲

In the end, the president of the United States didn't need to agonize over making the next difficult decision. It was already made for him. Darci had just revealed to him the most incriminating secret about his political campaign that he never expected her to know. The silence in the Oval Office was unbearable, and she was waiting for an answer. He stared at her across his desk, utterly at a loss for words. She was blackmailing him.

It started innocently enough when she requested an urgent private meeting before his next conference with Tate and his team. He accepted, nonchalantly thinking it was a debriefing about the reactions from several departments in the city they were all accountable to.

"You can't be serious," the president stammered.

Darci had not flinched when she went down the list of the gory details. He knew she had a closet full of skeletons. She had something on everyone in this city, but he had not expected her to pull one on him.

"Believe me, I am extremely serious," Darci said. "And you should be more scared of your wife finding out than the general public."

"You would risk our careers?"

"I'll go there if I have to. I'll tell the media everything," Darci said.

"You are adding to the impeachment threat being demanded by the public by exposing my personal business? You know that would destroy me," the president angrily replied.

"I know it's been tough lately," Darci stated, "but too many lives are at stake if you go through with the second round of your plan."

"What's your request?"

"All I want is time. Specifically, one hour," Darci said as she got up to leave.

"You expect me to tell Tate to hold off for one hour, when we've already set everything in motion? Any moment now the corrupted code could get into the cloud. That would mean the destruction of Chicago and then move to other cities. We are looking at an epidemic here," he grumbled.

"I'm sure you will think of something," Darci said, serenely. "One hour."

CHAPTER 18

Chase swung the ax with all his strength. The blade arced through the air, striking the beam with a tremendous *thwack*. The beam split, clearing the way for Ashlynn to be pulled up to safety. Chase leaned on the ax, both hands on his knees, willing the throbbing pain in his side to subside.

Ashlynn was even more desperate to be free now. She pulled at her leg, clearly panicked.

"Hey, calm down," Mindy said.

"I…I can't feel my leg anymore," Ashlynn said in a panic-stricken voice.

"Darling," Mindy said as she wiped sweat from Ashlynn's brow, "we'll get you out."

Max then came up to snuggle as close as possible to Ashlynn; that seemed to calm her down. Enough for Mindy to feel around Ashlynn's leg; it was still firmly trapped.

"Chase," she said, "we're going to need that ax one more time."

Ben sped down the road toward the airstrip, abandoned cars and other debris littering the way before them. Ben had to swerve to avoid a tree trunk, Scott ducking instinctively, expecting the worst, but Ben kept the car in control.

"Know anything about the Eaglefly?" Ben asked.

"Eaglefly T-four. Built in 2010. Seats two. It was grounded before it took to flight. Another model won out for mass production." Scott effortlessly rattled off the facts.

"Very good, but you're wrong on the last point," Ben corrected. "It's been flown several times by a crazy genius: my dad, whom you're about to meet. Best thing about that plane? It flies under radar. That's why no one knows anything about it other than that it's sitting in some hangar collecting dust."

The antique plane landed and came to a stop. Ben and Scott stepped out of the shadows and walked up as its engines shut off.

Jesse Knight stepped out. He looked as eccentric as the old plane. In his sixties, he was an ageless, silver-haired Iron Man. Jesse had been one of the original pilots for the plane and had found a way to keep the prototype for his use. Jesse wasn't pleased to see Ben was meticulously checking out the plane, but he knew better than to stop his son.

Scott whistled in awe at the antiquated object. How Ben's father got a hold of it was a story Scott was dying to find out.

"You flew this?" Scott asked in amazement.

"How do you think it got here? It's a beauty, isn't it?"

Jesse unplugged the gas cap, let the gas drain out, and then patted the solar panels attached to the wings.

"The stored solar supply should get us close enough," Jesse said.

Scott licked his lips nervously. He had never gotten used to jumping out of good solid planes, and this one did not even fit the category.

"Is it safe?" Scott asked nervously.

"I didn't know I was supposed to babysit," Jesse answered. "I may charge a fee."

"Let's go," Ben urged.

"Before I forget…" Scott said, and turning to Ben, he continued, "You'll need these."

Scott handed him a laser injector along with his badge.

"You left your badge on your desk."

"How did you get into the safe?"

"Let's just say it's a skill acquired from my father. He was another old genius."

Ben was speechless; then he burst out laughing, shaking his head in amazement before pocketing the items with a quick thanks. Ben suspected that Scott was a 3-D expert and would have easily made a copy of his finger-prints. He made a mental note to ask how he did it when this was over.

The plane took off, flying dangerously low over the trees before increasing altitude. Both men put on their Brain Interface Caps and secured their parachutes. As they approached the field, Ben motioned to Scott to crawl over to the opposite side of the hatch and wait for the signal from Jesse.

"This is the closest I can get you," Jesse shouted.

He pressed a series of buttons that opened the hatch door. The two men held on tightly as the wind rushed in, and then Ben gave the thumbs-up signal and jumped. Scott took a deep breath and followed. The plane banked sharply and disappeared above them.

Henry marched into the field station fit to be tied.

"Anyone here care to tell me where Ben is?" he demanded.

The lack of response didn't surprise Henry. He would let it go for now and turned to Taylor.

"I want to see a status report every ten minutes."

Taylor rolled her eyes.

Ben landed lightly, dropping down onto the wet grass. He quickly pulled away from the chute and wrapped it up in record time. Scott, however, landed hard; his inexperience clearly showed as he tripped over his own feet. The chute fell over his head blinding him and causing him to stagger around as he got increasingly entangled. Ben raced after him, pulling him down to avoid detection. They walked briskly to Wrigley Field, coming around the corner to Clark Street.

Ben pulled Scott back when he saw two Robomen.

"What are they doing here?" Ben said. "This area is unassigned."

"Maybe they're psychic," Scott quipped. "Maybe they know their boss is here and have come to help him out?"

As they watched, one of the Robomen pulled away the ivy on the ground, exposing a trapdoor. It was one of the emergency exits to the underground tunnels beneath the stadium, used by dignitaries and celebrities who wished to keep away from prying eyes.

The Robomen slid down the tunnel and disappeared into the darkness.

Ben's face turned white. "Where did you say the signal you picked up in the stadium came from?"

Ben knew the answer even before Scott responded. It had been right in front of him all this time. He knew why the Robomen were heading into the stadium.

"Oh my God!" he gasped. "JR. He downloaded the offline file."

"How is that even possible?" Scott said.

"Yesterday at breakfast"—he nodded incredulously—"he wanted to play a game with me and sent it to my phone. It must have contained an agent that downloaded the data I was working on."

Ben scrambled to his feet.

"Where are you going?" Scott asked.

"What does it look like? My family's in danger."

"Those Robomen will destroy you."

"You can't stop me."

"Oh yes, I can."

Scott pulled Ben back, but Ben pushed him away and kept on running. Scott mustered all his energy and with surprising strength, tackled Ben to the ground. With his breath knocked out of him, Ben kicked against Scott and heard a grunt of pain.

"Ben, listen to me."

Ben growled.

"Think. You are not going to save your family by rushing in without a plan. Whoever sent the Roboman could be watching us right now."

Ben stopped fighting and fell back laughing hysterically.

"I can save the world, but I can't save my family," Ben said bitterly.

"Listen, I can disable them," Scott said. "Give me a couple of minutes."

Ben was emotionally spent. "You think the Robomen are going to go over and politely ask my family to hand over the file? My family doesn't have two minutes."

"Point taken. One minute."

Ben kept his gaze on Scott, tapped his jacket to activate his phone, and barked into his shoulder.

"Taylor."

⋏

Taylor looked up on her screen to see the incoming call, which she hastily activated.

"Where are you?"

She turned her back on Andre, who feigned disinterest, but Taylor knew he was all ears.

"It's miserable here," Taylor whispered. "Henry's driving me nuts. Your name's taboo around here, and Andre is getting creepy."

"I want you to do something in the system for me," Ben said.

"What do you need?" Taylor eagerly asked.

⋏

The two men sat close together to keep out of sight in the shadows of the silent road. Ben watched Scott's deft fingers fly over the minitablet, forcing himself to stay calm. Even with the years of training, this was not easy.

"You're making me nervous," Scott said.

"Your parents must be proud."

"They're dead."

"Sorry to hear that," Ben said, breathing slowly to keep himself calm.

"Don't be. They loved their reckless lives too much, I would say."

"What happened?"

"It's classified."

"Man, that would kill me, not knowing," Ben softly whistled.

"I didn't say I didn't know," Scott corrected.

Ben frowned. He was just about to ask a question when Scott shouted. "Eureka! I've got control. I have both of them in my sight."

"Good girl, Taylor," Ben said to himself, then to Scott, "Let's go."

⚔

Darci entered Dwight's office and closed the door softly behind her; then he walked around the room searching. She had grown suspicious of Dwight after their last conversation. Her eyes settled on the photo of Dwight laughing with the foreign delegates. She picked it up and studied it for a while before placing it carefully back in its place.

CHAPTER 19

Inside the tunnel, Ben and Scott followed the Robomen who were well ahead of them. Scott picked up, and they hurried to catch up. Once in a while, the Robomen would stop to scan the area before moving on.

"You can freeze them anytime, you know," Ben whispered to Scott.

"I must have damaged my cap when I made my smooth landing. I can't get the signal in the right place," Scott said, disgusted.

"Take my cap," Ben offered, starting to undo the strap.

"It'll take too long to reset. I'll try to do it real time in the cloud."

Scott typed on the computer and then stopped.

"What?" Ben asked.

"They've split up? One's taken a detour."

"Why?"

"Don't know. It's like someone was expecting me to track them down and knew how I was going to set it up. Like I said before, we may be walking into a trap."

"We can't change our plan now. We're running out of time. We'll deal with the other one later. Stay with the one ahead of us. I'll get close to this one and give you a line of sight. The server won't know the difference."

"It's too much power," Scott said. "You'll become a conduit, and your cap, including your head, will roast in seconds."

Taylor frowned over her screen while Andre watched her.

"What am I missing?" she asked of herself.

Andre grinned cynically. He watched the blinking light on his screen as he held down one key on his keyboard.

"Ah, I need to unlock the handle, of course," Taylor said.

Taylor typed and smiled with satisfaction.

"There."

Andre frowned. She'd won that round, but there were many more to come.

$$\lambda$$

In the tunnel, Scott scratched his head in surprise.

"Wait, I'm *in!* Taylor must have unblocked it."

The Roboman came to a full stop and powered down.

"You have twenty seconds to get ahead of it," Scott announced. "Go."

$$\lambda$$

Chase carefully wedged the blade of the ax in the space between Ashlynn's leg and the rubble while Mindy wrapped her arms around Ashlynn's upper leg, steadying her as carefully as possible. JR wrapped his arms around her chest ready to pull as instructed by Mindy.

"Ready?" Chase said.

Ashlynn's chin quivered, but she nodded bravely. Chase strained with all his might against the ax, pushing the rubble away from her leg. After a tense moment, the rubble yielded, and Mindy pulled Ashlynn's leg free.

Ashlynn felt the pain shoot up her leg all the way to the top of her head, then screamed, and passed out.

"Ashlynn," Mindy cried.

Chase doubled over with his hands on his knees. Sweat poured from his forehead, and his side was throbbing intensely. He had to take control of the pain quickly before the others saw his state and became alarmed. Taking a deep breath, he slowly stood up.

$$\lambda$$

Ben raced down the hallway toward the still Roboman. Twenty seconds were more than enough to get ahead of the machine, but as he drew closer and as if sensing his presence, it lit up, turned, and walked toward him. Ben stopped in his tracks.

"I thought you said twenty seconds!" Ben called out to Scott.

Ben looked around for a quick option while Scott desperately typed.

"Hang on," Scott called out.

Ben backed away, but he knew it was hopeless. He slowly pulled out the laser injector.

At the field station, Taylor could see that she was blocked again. She looked at Andre, but he seemed engrossed in his work. Maybe she was making it too complicated.

"Let's try going in through the front door," she muttered as she rapidly typed.

The Roboman was still moving toward Ben.

"Scott?" Ben said, trying to stay as calm as possible.

He could hear Scott typing frantically and felt like he was nothing more than a spectator to this unavoidable disaster.

To keep his mind off things, Ben did what he would do in a military setting—he studied the Roboman. Something looked familiar about this one. He scanned the machine, looking over every detail in his usual meticulous way. Then his face cleared with recognition. The Roboman had four fingers on his right hand. It was missing a pinky.

"Hello, Slade," Ben said.

To which Scott gave a confused look.

"It has a name?"

Taylor stared at the monitoring graphs on her screen.

"Not again! The system's stalling," Taylor exclaimed.

Andre nonchalantly worked on while Taylor typed with determined ferocity.

"I can bypass the local PLC and go directly to the virtual one…"

Taylor pressed the Enter key and then chuckled. "I'm good."

Andre frowned.

⋏

At the tunnel, Scott shook off the sweat and pressed the Enter key. This time, the download bar went all green.

"Yes!" Scott yelled.

Ben turned on the laser injector as Slade drew near.

"Hold on, Ben," Scott called out. "I'm almost in."

"You're out of time," Ben said, watching Slade playfully circle around him.

Scott was still struggling to come to the right solution but wasn't fast enough.

"Just don't use the injector," Scott said, "not yet. Remember, I need this one to update the code."

Then Slade slammed against Ben, sending the laser injector flying. Man and machine were locked in a death grip. With one effortless move, Slade lifted Ben up. Ben hovered midair for a second then slammed down to the ground. His eyes rolled to the back of his head, but he fought against the blackness. He tracked the injector and scrambled toward it, but Slade pulled him back, raising him up again. Once again, he felt the hard impact of the ground.

"Come on!" Scott screamed at the computer.

Slade scooped Ben up again, locked him in a death grip, and squeezed. Ben screamed, writhing in pain against the monster.

Scott pounded the keyboard; this time Slade froze. Ben slid out of its grip and down to the ground.

"Hello, Slade. You've been had." Scott grinned. "Care to take a turn with me?"

Ben sucked in a breath, slowly got up, and wiped the blood off his face. He picked up the laser injector and checked the time.

"I can take care of the other one, too," Scott assured him.

Ben was already on the run. He checked his watch. The hour was almost over. "There's no time. You need to speed the Robomen up, now. I'll deal with this one. Don't worry about me."

"You're the boss," Scott acknowledged.

⋏

Mindy and Chase secured the homemade splint on Ashlynn's leg as gently as possible while Ashlynn bravely stifled her groans. The leg was badly bruised and possibly broken in multiple places. Chase handed her the last couple of painkillers, which she took gratefully.

"JR, you can send Daddy a message now," Mindy said.

JR had barely reached for the jacket to pull out the phone, when he was distracted by a noise down the hallway. JR looked over his fortress and began to tremble. His booby trap had worked, but just for a second.

"Guys?" JR said. "There's a Roboman coming this way."

Mindy was not taking a chance finding out if it was programmed for good or if it was one of the rogues.

"Get down to the closet, now," Mindy ordered.

"Maybe it's okay." Chase hoped.

"We don't want to find out if it isn't," Mindy said. "Go!"

The family ran down the hallway toward the closet. Max stood his ground ready to defend the family, but JR was not about to see his friend sacrificed, even for his family.

"Come on, Max," shouted JR.

The Roboman kicked away JR's makeshift defense and headed toward the closet. Meanwhile, Mindy and JR ran into the closet, followed by Chase carrying Ashlynn. Once everyone was in, Mindy slammed the door shut. Max barked and jumped at the closed door.

Chase carefully put Ashlynn down. JR fought to hold down Max, but Max continued to bark wildly as he struggled to get free. Mindy locked the door and with trembling hands took the phone from her pocket.

"I'm going back," Chase said.

"Don't move," Mindy warned.

"Mom, I can skate away from here, and it'll come after me, and you'll be safe," Chase said.

But Max was not to be outdone; he barked wildly and leapt at the door.

"Let Max go," Mindy said.

"No!" JR wailed.

"It'll give us time. JR, we have to save Ashlynn," Mindy said.

JR released Max, and Mindy opened the door. Max rushed out. Chase tried to leave, but with the strength only a mother could muster, Mindy blocked him, shoving him back into the room as she locked the door.

"Mom!" Chase cried.

Mindy turned around and hugged her children.

"I love you."

She tapped the phone to send the text to Ben.

In the hallway, Max crouched down, baring his teeth at the Roboman, defending the door. Growling, Max sprung forward and attacked the Roboman, but Max was swatted aside with one swing from a massive arm. The dog yelped as he took a short flight in the air and landed in an injured heap. The Roboman grabbed the closet door handle and pulled hard.

Surprisingly, the door held. Chase had jammed a chair under the door handle and pushed a storage cupboard against the door.

⋏

Ben sprinted through the tunnel, eyes searching ahead. Was he too late? Adrenaline drove him on. He saw Mindy's message at the same time he heard a dog's yelp.

Suddenly, he saw Max, who weakly barked his greetings, and then he saw the Roboman at the closet door.

The Roboman coiled up, preparing for a second and final kick.

"Hey!" Ben shouted.

To Ben's relief, the Roboman turned toward him and away from the door. He knew he would have a slight advantage if he could cause the robot to hesitate for even a nanosecond. It would give him a chance to get the injector in the most vulnerable part of its neck for a fast destruction. Ben rushed at the Roboman, heaving his whole body forward into the machine. He kicked at the vulnerable gap above the Roboman's knee hoping to send the Roboman stumbling, but the machine did not budge.

Ben felt the all-too-familiar metal fingers curl around his neck and then tighten instantly into an iron grip, and he grunted in pain. His knees buckled under him, his eyes popping. Fighting against the blackness, he flicked the laser injector on and focused on the Roboman's neck. His hands were shaking so badly he could barely position the injector, but he willed himself to focus on just that one point in front of him. In one fluid move, he jabbed the injector down the Roboman's neck.

The result was instant. The Roboman shook violently as its entire AI computer core roasted. In a moment it went limp, dropping Ben as it thudded to the ground.

Ben fell down to his knees, clawing at his neck and wheezing.

"Leave my family alone," Ben croaked. Spent, he leaned back against the wall until he got enough breath to pull himself up.

Ben pounded loudly on the door.

"Mindy, Chase! It's me."

No one inside the closet could hear Ben's shouts or Max's weak barks. Ashlynn was crying uncontrollably, and JR was screaming. Chase flung himself against the door.

Mindy heard the pounding on the door above the noise, but it was different from the metallic clunks of the machine.

"Quiet guys," Mindy urgently said, "listen!"

Ben continued to pound on the door, shouting out the names of his family.

"It's Dad!"

Chase pulled away the chair and flung the door open. The two men looked at each other.

"You all right?" Ben inquired.

Chase nodded.

"Ashlynn needs a doctor," he announced and then crumbled to the floor.

⋏

Outside the stadium, Slade stood silently by as Scott pressed the Execute key on his computer, completing the transfer of code into the Robomen, and then looked at Slade.

"Tell them up there that I send my best regards."

Slade's eyes lit up, his head turning up. A beam shot straight upward from his head into the sky.

In the stratosphere, the ERC satellite went into overdrive. In turn, back on Earth, in the center, the Roboman servers updated and transmitted the information on the machines. Confused, the techs stepped back. All around the disaster areas in Chicago, the Robomen froze for a brief moment, and then their movement increased. Faster, then faster still, and in that moment, the face of the entire rescue operation changed.

CHAPTER 20

Taylor couldn't believe her eyes. The red-zone areas on the screens were rapidly changing to green. The Robomen were working twice as fast. There were no more rogues. All were functioning as commanded, so she quickly ran tests to make sure.

"Henry, look at this," Taylor said, breathless with excitement.

But Henry wasn't paying attention. He had finally located the Knight family.

"Not now. I found Ben," Henry called back. "We just picked up a signal from his son's phone."

"Look!" Taylor insisted, rambling a bit in her elation. "They're moving... as commanded and much faster."

"What?" Henry gasped, turning quickly around. "Who did this?"

"Who cares!" Taylor laughed. "We're back in business."

Andre was visibly shaken and sat down quickly to disguise his weakened knees. Up until now, he had been confident of his concealed methods. The complicated paths and distractions he set up masked the original machine and ensured, if discovered, that Ben would be implicated. He mulled over the idea of setting another trap but immediately decided against it. It was better to wait. Nothing had been discovered yet that would point to him. He was sure Ben could not defeat the trap he had set. There could only be one answer: Scott!

λ

Darci checked her phone for what seemed like the hundredth time, pacing back and forth outside the conference room. There were no messages from Ben. She was trying her best to stay optimistic, but time was running out. She kept checking the charts for any changes in the analysis. They were only showing more dysfunctional behavior from the machines. The situation was becoming dire, and President Nelson had already ordered the countdown to begin.

The bomber was almost on top of the stadium, the Captain already locked in on the target area.

"Stand by," he said. "Twenty seconds."

Darci knew she had to go back into the conference room and watch the destruction with the rest of the group. She wouldn't flinch in front of everyone, but she was dying inside.

She opened the door just as her phone buzzed.

⅄

Darci burst into the conference room, automatically drawing frowns from all over the room.

"Call it off," she shouted.

She pointed her phone to the wall, and a picture of working Robomen came up.

"Our Robomen are working just fine. In fact, they've never been better. The corrupted code has been removed. There's no trace of it anywhere."

⅄

Back in Chicago, the hot air from the helicopter wiped the grass flat as it landed on the field outside the stadium. Ashlynn and Chase were on stretchers being loaded onto the aircraft, while Ben handed JR's phone to Scott before he climbed in.

"This is what they were after," Ben shouted above the noise. "I don't know how the kid downloaded the data, but he deserves to be grounded for a year."

"I'll put back the missing data; it will be like it never left," Scott said. "The agent that was in JR's game could be a dormant one, judging from what hasn't happened yet. I'll find and remove it before its owner realizes the treasure it's sitting in."

"You know Andre did this," Ben sighed.

"He's just the little fish. I'll find Suspect Zero," Scott assured him. "He, or it could be a she, would have been communicating with Andre through some means, and I can find the digital fingerprint that I can trace all the way back to the one behind this all."

"He's probably deleted everything by now?" Ben asked.

"Then I'll just undelete it all," Scott shrugged. "The only real way to protect an electronic file from being found by a guy like me is to burn the hard drive with actual fire. If Suspect Zero kept any incriminating correspondence or other evidence on his computer at *any* point in time at all, then I'll be able to uncover it, no matter *how* good he thinks he's deleted it. Then I'll just flag everything for the right people to find."

"I know you will. If it's Henry—" Ben began as he got into the helicopter.

"I'll be gentle," Scott shouted, "I promise. It shouldn't take me long."

He crunched down to avoid the swirling dust blast as the helicopter lifted off.

Chapter 21

Ashlynn shrieked with joy as her grandpa spun her round and round in her wheelchair in the hospital visitor's area. Her leg was in a cast, but she couldn't be happier to be free and alive. JR engaged them in a pretend gun battle, while Max, with his legs bandaged, thumped his tail slowly to show his approval.

A few doors away, Ben and Mindy gazed at Chase as he slept in his hospital bed. Ben smiled at Mindy.

"When we were in the basement, I was so scared I would never see you again," Mindy told him.

"You don't have to worry about that ever again," he assured her as he leaned over to kiss her. "I'm not going anywhere; I'm staying right here."

"Guys..." Chase said as he sleepily stirred, "get a room."

Mindy laughed; Chase was going to be all right.

"Look who's back with us." Ben grinned.

"Dad," Chase said as he struggled to sit up, "you gotta go...stop them..."

Ben gently pushed him back against the pillows.

"Shhhh, you need to rest," he said, trying to calm Chase down.

"That Roboman was going to kill us."

"He's delirious," Mindy said to Ben.

"I'm not. Do something, Dad. Don't let them kill."

"The Robomen are all right now," Ben said.

"No one's better than you, Dad. You have to stop them," Chase urgently insisted. "What if something goes wrong again? People will die."

Chase was right. People were still trapped, and anything could go wrong even after Scott changed the code.

Mindy and Ben exchanged a look. She knew her husband too well.

"Go," she said. "It's the right thing."

But Ben shook his head.

"I won't say it again," she insisted. "People need you; now go."

Ben gave Chase a pat on the head and then gave Mindy a kiss.

"Be careful," Mindy whispered.

Ben smiled and headed out the door.

⚔

It took everything in Andre's power to fake a relaxed expression when Scott walked into the room and sat down at a workstation that directly faced him. He feigned a deep concentration looking at the monitoring systems, but it was a cover to watch Scott's every move. On the inside Andre was boiling with rage. His world was knocked off-kilter, when Scott walked into the room yesterday. Yet, the challenge of beating this enemy raised his adrenaline level, and he welcomed it.

He glanced up at Scott, meaning to hold his gaze, but as soon as Scott looked up, he glanced away. Courage he possessed in spades, but he had to be careful not to incriminate himself by making a stupid move. For now, he would hack into Scott's computer and get ready to block his work in the cloud. The race was on. It was geek versus geek. His stomach growled, reminding him he had not eaten any real food for hours. How he longed for a juicy burger, he was so tired of eating algae chips.

Scott started his search for clues about Slade. He started with the easiest search and entered the model and its identity number. A code ran past his view, giving the expected public company information, but tracking and other analyses about the Robomen were classified. He then ran a deep dive on it but came up with nothing.

Scott paused to think. He had succeeded in speeding up the Robomen, but the risk of the rogue code getting into the cloud was still high because the mole was still on the loose, and anything could happen any second.

It was time to go through the back door. He inserted a flashcard into the computer.

Watching him, Andre frowned.

A network page came up on Scott's monitor. He was in!

"Eureka!" he said.

Andre eyed Scott nervously across the room and felt a tightening in his stomach. He had managed to stop the first deep dive but could not detect where Scott was going next. He would have to set up more firewalls. He knew he was dealing with a mastermind, and this was not going to be easy. But he too had tricks up his sleeve.

Scott hit the Enter button.

On Scott's screen, the download bar quickly loaded, but stopped halfway.

"Not again," Scott groaned.

Andre breathed a sigh of relief. He took full advantage of the break and typed rapidly to set up more obstacles.

On Scott's screen, a spider moved rapidly across the line of code. Scott scanned the code, methodically going over each line, stopping the cursor on the kill date. It was 10-27-2051. He then continued on down the lines of code.

The download bar reached 80 percent and froze.

Andre cracked a slow smile and whispered under his breath, "Not too clever, are you?"

Undeterred, Scott typed again.

The download bar started up again. Now it was Andre's turn to type frantically, but too late. The download continued to 100 percent complete. Scott pulled out the flashcard and logged off in the nick of time.

"Gotcha!"

Andre jabbed at the Delete key again and again, but as he already knew, it was too late. He felt nauseated. What had gone wrong?

⋏

Taylor was frustrated. She wasn't getting much help from Andre. How could he be so preoccupied during the biggest event of both their lives. Just doing good work was not good enough; she wanted to please Ben. The mall was the last place to clear; she felt like all her success would come to a screeching halt if she was unable to provide a safe passage to the people trapped there. In previous years, the building had received some earthquake reinforcement, but the public had voted to keep its original walls intact, making it a national treasure and a great tourist attraction for the city. Most of the floors had collapsed, and the walls kept shifting, causing the Robomen to rapidly change rescue routes as passages kept getting unstable or blocked. At times, she even had to manually reposition the train tracks for the trolleys. The pillars in the middle of the mall began to crack and would crumble in minutes. Most of the people were on the eighth floor where the shoe sale and Brandon Bosk's show had been in full swing. The exits were destroyed, and the stairs were dangerously cracked or missing. The Robomen had set up temporary pillars from the first floor to the ceiling to keep the walls intact for as long as possible.

Taylor requested a self-replication rail over a big gap between the floors, but a lever had got stuck, and the trolleys filled with people had come to a halt. Panic began to set in. The pillars could not hold the structure forever, and the walls had started crumbling.

"Andre," Taylor called out, "I need some help here."

"The lever's stuck," Andre announced, stating the obvious. "I'm sending a Roboman to shift the rail. I'll guide it through the process."

"There's not enough time," Taylor replied.

Despite instructions to stay in the trolleys, the people climbed out looking for another escape route.

She couldn't bear to look. Feeling despair, she turned her head just in time to catch a glimpse of Ben running toward the people.

"Hurry. Get back into the trolleys. You'll die if you don't!"

"Taylor, tilt it to the other side," she heard Ben shout.

"I can't; the trolleys will roll over."

"Just do it!"

Ben located the malfunctioning lever of the railroad and pulled with all his might. The trolleys moved a little and stopped. He kicked the lever and pulled, straining hard. The rail shifted, and much to the relief of the survivors, the trolleys moved, connecting safely down to the seventh floor then to the sixth. Parts of the ceiling were continuing to crumble.

"Speed the trolleys up, Taylor," Ben called out.

"They're at maximum speed," Taylor replied. "The extra strain will split them apart."

"I don't care how you do it, just get the people down to the first floor and out."

Ben looked up and spotted the singer struggling to free himself from the rubble on the eighth floor. He raced up the stairs, leaping over the gaps. Ben pulled Bosk from the rubble and pushed him into the trolley.

Ben then rushed back to see if anyone else was trapped, but the roof was collapsing all around him. The earth shook.

"Ben, get out of there," Taylor wailed.

He turned and raced after the trolley leaping to grab on to the back of it.

⋏

A huge aftershock rocked the city. A sinkhole opened and swallowed the Eyeball monument; skyscrapers strained and groaned, and older buildings tumbled in a cloud of dust. The honeycomb of tents in the bamboo village shifted and shook but stayed upright. Inside them, people screamed as they were tossed from side to side.

A jolt knocked Taylor off her chair.

The shaking stopped. The last trolley spun around and came to a stop. It had just cleared the building. The people were delirious with joy that they had made it out alive. Then from the chaos of dust and debris, Ben walked out into view. The techs all high-fived and cheered.

"Commence Phase Two," the Logistics Robot announced.

"Great work everyone!" Ben called out for all to hear.

Henry clasped his head in disbelief.

"Forty-eight hours!" Henry announced. "Unbelievable."

⋏

Darci indulged President Nelson with a warm handshake.

"Congratulations, Mr. President," Darci said and smiled. "Not a second too soon."

"Incredible," he replied. "For a moment, I thought we weren't going to make it."

Darci checked her buzzing smartphone, summarizing what it told her as she read from its screen. "The phones are ringing off the hook. Even Fontini, who'd been pouting for months, sent a congratulatory message on behalf of Italy."

"That old hat. He never calls without asking for money."

"And this would be the perfect excuse."

They chuckled. The president could not resist a jab at Darci.

"Don't you regret your decision?" he asked.

"To drag you through the mud?" she smirked. "Not for one millisecond."

"I didn't think so." He sighed.

In his office, Dwight stared at his hands resting on his lap. His phone buzzed, and he picked up it up.

"Dwight Ellison," he said.

There was absolute silence.

Dwight put down the phone. His head sank into his chest. He had to come to terms with what he knew would be disastrous ramifications if any evidence led to him. To make matters worse, he still wasn't any closer in finding out what Darci knew. Finding out would've given him an advantage and helped him get out of this mess. But now, it was probably a good idea to start closing out accounts and emptying his drawers. He was going to make sure it wasn't his head on the block. Everything still pointed to ERC.

Just then he glanced up at the photo on his desk. A hand-drawn smiley face in black ink over his image stared back at him.

Chapter 22

Taylor nodded off at her desk while Scott and Henry helped themselves to coffee. Andre shifted his weight, agitated. Ben entered giving Scott a knowing look; to Ben's relief, Scott shook his head.

Henry put down his coffee when he saw Ben.

"About last night—" he started.

But Ben stopped him.

"I would've done the same."

They both nodded; all was forgiven.

"Shall we start the debrief? I'm sure you all want to go home," Henry stated.

"Absolutely," Ben said. "I'll begin."

He turned to Andre who shuffled uncomfortably.

"Why did you do it?" Ben accused.

"Do what?" Andre said, trying to sound self-assured. "I don't understand."

Taylor's head snapped up. She was instantly wide awake.

"What's going on?" she asked.

"Let me elaborate. Slade."

Andre swallowed uncomfortably.

"Where are you going with this, Ben?" Henry said, impatiently.

Ben walked slowly toward Andre. "Muyang was your trial run, wasn't it?"

"Dude," Andre snapped, "I don't know what you're talking about."

He licked his dry lips trying his best to control his anxiety and at the same time furious that he'd shown even a hint of fear.

"You switched Slade's code in Muyang to test your plan."

"What?" Henry gasped.

Andre backed away from Ben. "Don't listen to him, Henry," Andre said as he backed away from Ben. "It's pure nonsense. He stole data, and now he's trying to cover it up."

"The Muyang data sync?" Ben said.

"That's right. It's gone and...you took it so...so you can sell it on the black market to the highest bidder," Andre stammered.

"Do you mean"—Scott pressed the Enter key on his virtual keyboard, and lines of code filled the screens on the walls—"this data? As you can all very well see, it shows one hundred percent of the residential evidence of Muyang before someone took a generous helping to someone else's property."

Andre looked around for an escape. He grabbed Taylor, shielding himself with her body, put her in a headlock, and whipped out a knife ready to shove it into her neck.

"Hey, what are you doing?" Taylor uttered in surprise.

Andre wrapped his arm around her and pulled her to his chest, the knife poised at her throat. Ben could see that Andre was desperate enough to be really dangerous and moved not a step closer.

"You can't prove anything," Andre said.

"Who are you really working for?" Ben asked.

"You sabotaged our operation?" Henry put in.

"Stop! Let go of me," Taylor cried out as she struggled against the iron grip.

"I would do what she says," Scott said in a threatening tone.

"I won't. I love you, Taylor," Andre told her. "I did this for you."

"Then why are you holding a knife to my neck? A bit melodramatic, don't you think?"

"If I can't have you, no one can," Andre cried out. "Why did you have to go and fall in love with Ben? I was doing this all for you, and you ruined everything."

"So you wanted to destroy him, and it almost worked," Scott summed up as he moved slowly toward Andre.

Andre tightened his grip. "You come any nearer, and I kill her," he snarled, his eyes darting from one man to the other.

Everyone froze. Taylor whimpered.

"You got lazy and used a premade rootkit," Scott said carefully. "Or you just couldn't write one as good. Again, I commend you for choosing the best, but rule number one for a worm: always build your own rootkit."

Andre clenched his teeth. Meanwhile, Ben was edging closer to Andre, unnoticed.

"Don't," Andre snorted with bravado.

"The least you could've done was change the kill date," Scott scoffed. "A good hacker never forgets his kill date."

Ben came from behind and knocked the knife away, startling Andre, who he then hit on the side, spinning him away from Taylor.

Ben stood over Andre, his eyes smoldering with anger. He threw a left hook, connecting with the younger man's jaw, and Andre dropped like a sack of potatoes.

"That's what you get for putting my family through hell," he said with a face full of fury.

It would be a while before Andre could move again.

CHAPTER 23

In his haste, Dwight tripped over his chair. He rummaged through his desk drawers, pulling out several flashcards and a gun, and then stuffed the items in his pockets.

It certainly wasn't money that drove Dwight toward espionage. He had plenty of that, and he had ways of getting more. He had no public scandals his excellent lawyers and bribed journalists could not deal with, so no one bothered to blackmail him. Ideology played a little part, but mostly it was his ego that drove him. The power he felt controlling the president's decisions was quite intoxicating, and he had come to believe his own hype. He felt invincible. So what if he decided to offer some secrets to his powerful friends outside the United States? It was a global world, and it was done for the greater good, a favor that could be returned at a critical time.

He regretted having trusted Andre with too much, underestimating his crazy love over a slinky scientist he wanted to impress. From the beginning, it had not been hard to entice him. Andre admired Dwight and perceived him as a father he never had, so he had been easy to manipulate and coax information out of. He had to admit he should have had Andre on a shorter leash but hadn't expected him to mess up so soon, or he would have disposed of him earlier.

There was a knock on the door, and an aide entered.

"Not now!" growled Dwight.

The aide backed away quickly and closed the door.

⋏

Air Force One was warming up for lift-off to Chicago, and the presidential entourage had already started boarding. On the tarmac, Dwight ran after Darci.

"You weren't leaving without me."

Darci ignored him and continued to walk.

"I won't apologize, Miss Woods," Dwight told her.

"Save it for your foreign bosses, you treasonous scum," Darci snapped. "You're on the payroll of several governments while holding a powerful position in the US government. Something you forgot to tell the Justice Department!"

Dwight stopped in his tracks. "Strong words, but you can't prove anything."

"You should erase your computer files a bit better," Darci said, catching him in the eyes with a harsh glare. "We discovered some rather incriminating evidence in your deleted files. You either got greedy or careless, while lobbying on behalf of a plethora of foreign governments."

Dwight's face turned white.

Inside Air Force One, Darci and Dwight took their seats opposite each other and strapped in. His plan had failed miserably, so it was time to make amends with her. Yes, he was an agent for a foreign power, but only if he was found out. Somehow, he had to find a way to salvage whatever he could and get back in the president's good graces. It was time to think and think hard.

"Let's start over. I'm willing to trade you anything you want. You name it," Dwight whispered, desperately hoping greed would work on Darci.

"How about the lives you took?" Darci said.

"Don't go saintly on me. Don't you see? I did it for our country."

"On the contrary," the president corrected as he entered in with his entourage, "your vicious snobbery and conspiracy to defraud the United States government almost took us down."

"Let me explain, sir," Dwight began.

"Quiet! Save it for your lawyers. You disgust me," the president snarled. "Get him off this plane. Just be glad we haven't left the ground yet!"

Two service men bore down on Dwight. He unstrapped slowly, eyes locked on Darci.

"Don't leave the country," Darci told him.

Dwight gritted his teeth and leaned toward Darci. It took all his will-power to speak softly.

"You've always envied my power over the president and coveted my position."

"Like I said before, Dwight, hope is an invaluable thing," Darci said with a slow grin. "Wouldn't you agree?"

Dwight could do little more than grumble to himself as he was very roughly escorted out.

CHAPTER 24

The sunshine slipped through the clouds over Chicago and washed over the crowd assembled in the front of the Shedd Aquarium. A wall of remembrance was to the side for all who wanted to pay their respects to the dead, while a Roboman stood majestically behind President Wolf Nelson as he addressed the gathering. The sound of grating faded in and out over the amplifiers, which were deliberately set not to drown out the president's voice but loud enough to show the listening world that the rebuilding of the city was in full swing.

Ben and his entire family, including Jesse, sat in the front row with Max keeping guard over JR. JR petted Max fondly, but it came with a price. His eyes watered, and he sneezed occasionally, but he couldn't be happier.

With all this strategically set as her backdrop, reporter Bly Cochrane stood before her camera making her statement to her audience.

"Secretary of State Dwight Ellison has resigned, taking full responsibility over the decisions that led to the tragic events at Wrigley Field…"

Meanwhile, President Wolf was just finishing up his remarks.

"…and now, Colonel Ben Knight," the president announced, "you have a medal to receive."

As Ben walked up to the podium, the crowd clapped even louder.

"Make the speech count, Ben," Henry muttered under his breath as the man passed him by. "We don't want to beg for funds ever again."

Ben stood before the president for a moment until the applause died down a bit; then the president picked up the medal and ribbon from an attending aide and turned to face him.

"Colonel Ben Knight, for actions that saved the lives of hundreds of people and uncovered a heinous plot to undermine the Roboman program for mere political gain, and for doing so in time to prevent a disastrous decision, it is with great pleasure that I award you this Presidential Medal of Freedom. Good work."

Applause once again arose as Ben bowed his head to permit the president to drape the medal around his neck, then a firm handshake with the president before he stepped back and left the podium to Ben. He stood there for several seconds, eyes scanning the crowds and picking out faces of gratitude here and there, not the least of which were the loving looks of his own family. He wasn't sure what he was going to say, not until he locked eyes with Mindy and saw the faith and love running down her face one tear at a time.

When he finally put up a hand for silence, he got it nearly immediately. Then he had the attentions of hundreds of people ready to focus on his every word, as well as the billions watching this live broadcast the world over. For the moment he was a celebrity, a hero; what he said now would be long remembered, whether he wanted it or not.

"I received this medal for saving lives, but the truth is that there was a whole team of people behind this medal. People, and the Robomen that we've designed and proven in the field. They work hard with one goal: to save lives. Not just the lives of people here in Chicago but lives everywhere, every country. They do it regardless of any personal considerations because they know that lives are the most precious of commodities. Lives that today included my own family, as well as the families of many others."

He paused briefly to glance over to where JR was holding Max and exchanged a brief smile before turning a more serious expression back to the audience.

"The Roboman program is an invaluable and cost-effective way of saving those lives, unlike any tool humanity has ever had before. Yet there are still some who would put a price on how many lives are worth saving with this tool or decide which lives might be more important than others. They would ask us to choose which little boy or girl to save, so they can have money enough for something else. To them I say this: Which one of your *own* children would you choose? Human life doesn't have a price tag or a budget. It has *value*. Thank you."

Ben's features were tense with emotion, try as he might to contain it, the crowd before him spotted through with many a damp face. He thought to back quietly off the stage, but the explosion of applause and cheers that greeted him kept him on stage longer than the speech itself had. A glance over to his wife showed her tearfully hugging their children while Henry was giving him two very enthusiastic thumbs up.

"No more begging," Henry was saying to himself. "No more funding hearings!"

It was a few minutes before he was finally able to walk down and lose himself from view behind the Wall of Remembrance, where a pleased-looking Darci met up with him.

"You still have it in you," she said.

"I know what you're thinking," he cautioned, deliberately looking over to his family. "Don't."

"Ahhh, civilian life." Darci sighed. "I guess some people actually have time for it."

"Nonnegotiable, I'm afraid," Ben replied. "Family life suits me just fine."

Then Darci looked over at Scott. Ben followed her gaze, his face softening.

"Do you think he knows?" Darci asked.

"He doesn't have a clue," Ben answered.

"He is not unhappy," Darci told him. "You did what you had to do to protect him."

"Let it go, Darci," Ben abruptly told her. "We can't turn back time, and we won't. I forgave myself a long time ago."

"Did you?"

Darci smiled when he didn't respond.

"So this is how you thank me! One day I'll need you. In this new world of clandestine security, you are never fully retired. For now, however, you'll excuse me. I've got to go clean up some loose ends."

Ben chuckled. "Don't you always?"

"Don't know what you mean..."

She laughed a hard and dry laugh as she walked away.

⚔

Scott stood apart from the crowd, watching the events with a bored look. His gaze settled on Taylor. She showed no sign of the ordeal she had faced a few hours ago but smiled as she chatted with people around her. Then she saw Ben turn to Mindy and whisper something in her ear, and Taylor's smile turned to plastic. Scott was surprised to feel a twinge of jealousy dart through him.

Scott sensed Darci approaching before he saw her.

"Once again, you've agitated the tectonic plates of nations—" Darci began.

Scott turned to face her, completing the sentence with no hesitation.

"The Moho boundary reveals its elusive self only for a moment," he finished.

Darci smiled with satisfaction.

"Maybe this time it will linger? Shall we walk? Glad to know you haven't forgotten your roots," she said. "Oh, and thanks for lighting up Dwight's computer files for us."

Scott shrugged and then followed her. Darci's aides lagged behind, but not too far. They stepped even further away at Darci's nod, giving her and Scott the privacy she needed.

"I have a job for you," Darcy told him. "The president makes his speech to the EU in a few hours. There's this one tedious issue that keeps cropping up—"

"The teleprompter hacker?" Scott grinned.

"Can you help?" Darci said.

Scott ignored her question. "You sent me that message in Vienna."

"Huh? What are you talking about?" Darci feigned ignorance.

"You knew I would get to the worm," Scott stated.

"It takes one to know one." She shrugged.

"You installed my rootkit in the ERC cloud, knowing Andre would take the bait and use it," Scott told her. "You bet on me remembering the kill date."

"You'd never forget the anniversary of your father's death," Darci stated. "He gave his life to save so many others who to this day have no idea what happened. But for those who did, we are forever grateful."

Scott looked away abruptly, while Darci's smile diffused the sadness.

"He was a hero. Will you take the job?"

"Why should I?" Scott replied.

"One," she listed, "you're wanted back in the United Kingdom. Your charges? Information espionage, intercepting messages, gambling away national security keys—"

"—Alleged, not confirmed," Scott interrupted her.

"Two," she continued, "hacking into His Majesty's Secret Service archives. For what? To look at your parents' records."

"Are you playing the family card already?" Scott playfully said.

"A few hotheads across the pond would love to get their hands on you."

"I'm not your property. You can't keep me here," Scott protested.

"We are not giving you back. You knew that the minute you stepped on that plane in Vienna, you would not be heading back to small spaces and bad weather any time soon."

The tension was cut when the audience clapped at the president's concluding statement. Darci and Scott joined the clapping. Taylor turned and caught Scott's eye, while Darci and Scott watched her as she made her way through the crowd.

"What makes you so sure I won't leave?" Scott teased.

"I told them you're wanted here for stolen code. Also, we're willing to provide a sweet substitute for you."

"Whoa, you're good, but I didn't steal the code."

"I know." She winked. "We too have our sources. Later?"

Darci turned to walk away, but Scott called after her.

"Wait. Why?"

"You can't escape what you are, Scott," she replied with her back turned. "It's in your blood. Deeply deceptive, but fiercely loyal. You have a good heart, like your father, and we want you on our side. ERC should keep you busy for a while until we need you."

"You loved him."

"Ahhh, love was never the issue. For you, however, there's still hope," she said looking at Taylor as she approached them. "Thank you for taking the job, by the way."

Scott looked at Darci as she walked away. He was surprised about her testament of love, but there was no time to ponder deeper as Taylor commanded his attention.

Scott and Taylor stared at each other for a long silent moment.

"You're not mad at me, are you?" Scott asked.

"I am, acutely," Taylor admitted. "I never thought it was possible to fix those dysfunctional Robomen, let alone speed them up so quickly."

"To think, it could have been implemented years ago," Scott told her. "You know I'm right, because you've read my white papers."

"I have to admit—you had great insight back then."

"And?"

"And what?"

"You're impressed?"

Taylor looked away, instinctively tracking down Ben and Mindy. "Maybe, but I'm still angry...bitter...still licking my wounds."

Scott took Taylor's face in his hands, blocking her view of the happy couple.

"Let me help with that. We shouldn't let the tyranny of the past cloud the future, should we?"

He then leaned forward and kissed her.

"Hey, stop!"

To her protest, he shut her up with another kiss.

"What were you saying?" Scott asked.

"N-nothing," Taylor purred.

Then she kissed him.

𝗔

Ben and Mindy walked hand in hand along the Wall of Remembrance. A bald eagle flew over them, closely followed by its mate. They looked up at the birds, then into each other's eyes and drew closer.

"My father once told me a story—" Ben said proudly.

"There you go again," Mindy chided, "talking about your dad. If I didn't know any better, I'd say you're trying to convince yourself that you love him. Sometimes I'm not even sure you know him that well."

Ben chuckled. "My father told me, when two eagles like each other, they fly together...forever."

"That's right, they make a home, together," Mindy said and nodded. "They spend time together as a family. You play with the kids and take out the garbage."

"Point taken." Ben laughed. "I told Henry under no circumstance should he even think of calling me anytime soon."

They looked deep into each other's eyes as the two eagles flew off over the Chicago skyline. The urgent message suddenly flashing across Ben's phone went completely unnoticed.

Up in orbit, the ERC satellite turned and sent a beam down somewhere over Europe, searching. There was a beep followed by a familiar rumble.

00:00:00...00:00:00...48:00:00